# REGULAR, SMEGULAR

## BECCA SEYMOUR

RAINBOW TREE PUBLISHING

# REGULAR, SMEGULAR!

## FAST BREAK
### BOOK 3

BECCA SEYMOUR

RAINBOW TREE PUBLISHING

# ALSO BY BECCA SEYMOUR

### ZONE DEFENSE

NO TAKE BACKS | NO MORE SECRETS | NO WRONG MOVES
| NO BACKING DOWN

### FAST BREAK

RULES, SCHMULES! | FACTS, SMACTS! | REGULAR SMEGULAR!
| EASY, SCHMEASY!

### TRUE-BLUE

LET ME SHOW YOU | I'VE GOT YOU | BECOMING US |
THINKING IT OVER | ALWAYS FOR YOU | IT'S NOT YOU |
OUR FIRST & LAST | NEXT FOR US

### OUTBACK BOYS

STUMBLE | BOUNCE | WOBBLE

### FANGS & FELONS

THICKER THAN WATER | WEAKER THAN INSTINCT |
BRIGHTER THAN FEAR

### STAND-ALONE CONTEMPORARY

NOT USED TO CUTE | HIGH ALERT | REALIGNED |
AMALGAMATED | UNDER THE BLAZING STARS | BEST KIND
OF AWKWARD

# AUTHOR'S NOTE

*Regular, Smegular!* is set in Georgia and uses both fictional and real locations and references. The timeline runs alongside the same period as Ty's book, *Facts, Smacts!* The basketball league in both the Zone Defense and Fast Break world is called the League, not the NBA. While I loosely followed the NBA structure, I created my own league and team names, my own competition names, and took liberties to make my fun, low-angst world work.

# CHAPTER 1
## LEON

The start of the school year is always kind of chaotic. Or more specifically, the prestart, since classes don't begin until Monday. I arrived at Brixham U a couple of days ago, wanting to settle in and catch up with my housemates before school begins and practice starts.

I plan to make the most of my senior year at Brixham. Not only by playing my ass off in basketball, but come next year, adulting begins.

I knock back the shot Sammy hands me, holding back my cringe. I'm not sure if the sour aftertaste of his gross concoction or the thought of working full-time causes the reaction.

"Leon, you want another?" Sammy grins and offers me a full shot glass. The contents of this one are red and gloopy-looking.

I scrunch my nose, undecided. I don't plan to get too wasted tonight, but if there was a night for it, this is it. It's probably my last chance of getting hard-core drunk. We'll meet with Coach in a few days, get our first look at the newbies, and I expect I'll receive an unforgiving reading list and class schedule.

Just the thought of the madness to come makes me nod and reach for the shot.

"Good man." Sammy clinks his glass against mine and downs it. While this one goes down easier, it's strong, and I'm pretty sure I've sprouted hairs on my otherwise smooth chest.

"Shit, Sammy, what the hell was in that thing?"

His snort doesn't reassure me. "You don't wanna know." He follows up with a wink before turning his attention to the brunette Bentley's talking to a few feet away.

Grinning, I leave him to it, swipe a beer from the counter, and work my way through the crowd.

Almost all my teammates are here tonight, which includes my four housemates. Other than Sammy and Bentley, I have no idea where the rest are, but that's more than okay. It's easy to get lost in the crowd, and at times like tonight, I like to blend in a little. That's not the easiest thing to do when the team is together. Sure, there's the whole height thing—we're pretty much giants among this crowd—but we also get loud and rowdy when together. So many personalities and big egos tend to make us one-up one another. It's fun, but tonight I just wanna go with the flow.

Maybe get my dick sucked.

I stop near the makeshift dance floor. It's full, with plenty of gyrating bodies to catch my attention. In theory. I glance around. There's no one I want to sidle up to. But that's okay. I've only been here an hour and am in no rush.

It's not like I'm looking for anything in particular. Honestly, a willing mouth will do.

Now, now, before you start wondering who this douche is—meaning me, obviously—I'm not that bad. I make it clear I'm just looking for a good, albeit quick time. It's also been a long, dry summer.

Taking another sip of my beer, I make my way around the outside of the crowd. A few people catch my eye, offering hellos or smiles. Each time, I grin back or give an up-nod. What I don't do is allow myself to get caught up in conversation.

Last season, our team, the Brixham Bears, kicked ass and won the playoffs. It means my face is recognizable. Not only on campus but in town and, honestly, to most discerning college basketball fans.

It's helped a lot to get no-strings-attached head, so I like the attention, but it sometimes gets exhausting. Did you know people can be fake as fuck? Go figure.

It's tiring to get bombarded by hangers-on who think I can give them street cred or an in if I go pro. That sounds all "woe is me," I know, but bear with me. People try to take advantage. People get in my space without an invite. It makes my whole no-strings head make more sense, right? Outside of my buddies, who are all my teammates, I don't trust anyone.

A round of cheers followed by hollers and laughter captures my attention. I follow the sound, curious that the noise broke through the pumping music. The journey takes me to a side room that, despite the volume, isn't crammed. There's probably fifteen people in the room, and I shit you not, they're playing spin the bottle.

I snort, mildly interested as the bottle spins. Seriously, I was fifteen the last time I played this game. I remember it, as Debbie Leicester shoved her tongue in my mouth, and to this day, I don't know how I stopped myself from gagging and humiliating her.

When the bottle lands on a couple of girls, my brows shoot up in surprise, and my mildly interested becomes a little more fascinated. Two girls making out... well, it's something different to look at. The group's reaction is like it was for the previous pair—a freckled redhead and skinny guy with specs.

It's kinda cool that they react the same. There's no sleazy comments, no lewd gestures or anything. I can't help but wonder if the reaction would be the same if it were guys kissing.

"You wanna play?"

It takes me a moment to realize the question is thrown my way. My gaze lands on the speaker, a brown-haired guy with longish hair and wearing an old-school Nirvana T-shirt—something I only recognize courtesy of my uncle. The guy indicates toward the space next to a blonde.

With a shrug, I make my way over. Why the hell not? Kissing can be fun, plus there's the whole adulting bullshit next year. When will I get the chance to do something so ridiculously immature again?

"Sure," I say, sitting my ass down, grinning at the round of applause and claps. "Anything I need to know?"

The same guy, who on my second look appears vaguely familiar, smirks and then quirks his brow. "Just that wherever the bottle stops, that's the person you're matched with. Tongues are optional, and on the mouth is essential." He bounces his brows, and a couple of people around the group chuckle. I join in and bob my head, not pulling away from the intensity of his dark gaze.

Do I have a problem if it lands on a guy? Not especially. Not that I've ever kissed a dude before, but have I thought about it? A time or five for sure. You can only hang out in a gay club so many times before your interest is piqued, right? Or is that just me?

Not that I go to gay bars for shits and giggles. It's always been doing my best-friend duty, with me and my housemates joining Kieran. He's one of my best friends, also our team captain, and over the years, when he's been looking to hook up, we've gone with him.

That's not as creepy as it sounds. We don't, like, watch him or anything. Well, not deliberately. But we have his back, have since the day we met, and there's no way we'd let him head into Atlanta without looking out for him.

I space out a little as the bottle spins, aware there's been some kissing. There's a couple of funny statements made, which are amusing, and when a guy to my right starts laughing about something Tiller said, I realize that's the name of the guy who invited me to join.

"A tongue piercing isn't the only one." Tiller's smirk is wide as he arches his brow. He tugs his tee, revealing ink on his pec and a bar through his nipple.

It's a struggle to pull my attention away. Ink and a nipple piercing… separate, they can be sexy, but together, they're hot as fuck. I've always thought that, whether on men or women. They look particularly spectacular on Tiller with his defined chest and washboard abs that I haven't failed to notice.

"It's the Prince Albert I'm curious about." The girl opposite me smirks, laser-focused on Tiller.

"Is that right?" Amusement colors Tiller's words while I flick my gaze down to his crotch.

Am I intrigued? Heck yes. I've always wondered what they look like in the flesh. No pun intended. Sure, I've seen photos, but the thought of seeing Tiller's dick, ideally when he's naked so I can see if the tattoos spread anywhere else, slams into my mind.

It's front and center and not going anywhere.

And fuck if my dick doesn't twinge in interest.

Again, not the first time this has happened. It is the first time, though, that my dick's reacting to a guy sitting within arm's reach of me and looking at me with barely concealed amusement.

Wide-eyed, I figure he's caught me staring at his junk. Heat burns my cheeks, and I glance away, trying to discreetly clear my throat while pulling up my knee, foot flat, to prevent any more awkwardness.

And by that, I mean this group getting an eyeful they never asked for of the boner growing in my pants.

The chick with short hair spins. Rather than focus on the bottle, I concentrate on how that means it's Tiller's turn next. My stomach dips at the thought, but it's not dread causing that reaction.

Awareness ripples through me. If the bottle lands on me, it means I get to kiss a guy—something I've been curious about for a while—but more than that, I get to kiss Tiller.

I have no idea who this man is, and despite seeming vaguely familiar, I can't for the life of me place his face. Regardless, he has my interest—100 percent of it, in fact.

Maybe it's because he hasn't said my name, made a big deal of knowing who I am. I don't say that because of my overinflated ego either. It's hard not to know I play for the Bears if you're a student here.

After the current kiss ends, I swallow hard and hold air in my lungs. I risk a glance toward Tiller. My breath whooshes out when his attention is already on me. With his head cocked, he seems to be studying me, and since I suck at hiding my reaction to him, a surge of "fuck it" slams into me.

I arch my brow at him. He can read into that whatever he wants. And then he spins. Rather than focusing on the bottle, I stare at him. His gaze doesn't drift either. We're caught up in this challenge of sorts, and I hope like fuck the bottle lands—

A squeal has me jerking my attention to the redhead. From the expression on her face—the goddamn glee there—I don't even have to look to know the bottle is pointed right at her. Hell, I would likely react the same way if the stupid bottle had singled me out.

I can't blame the girl.

I don't know if fascination or envy has me staring hard at her as Tiller leans across the space. A beat before their lips collide, his gaze snags mine. My chest tightens at that one look, and I can't watch. Glancing away, I focus on the window, which is a mistake as the reflection shows Tiller pressed against the girl.

And then it's over.

Is it me, or was that kiss super short? Like, a good ten seconds less than the others. Am I grasping? Maybe, but still, the cheering's died down, though there's plenty of laughter and talking, and the next spin has started.

But I don't really want to play anymore. It doesn't

matter that I haven't had my spin; the fun factor disappeared when I focused on the reflection.

"Your turn."

A nudge in my side startles me. The group's looking at me, and apparently, it's too late to make a run for it. Forcing a smile, I pick up the bottle. I may as well just get on with it.

I spin the damn thing and look away. At this point, I don't care who it lands on. A kiss is a kiss and isn't a big deal. Hell, I've lost count of how many kisses I've had over the years.

None of them have left a mark.

It's the sound of catcalls that alerts me to the bottle stopping. With a sigh, I peer down and focus on the bottleneck, my gaze traveling in its direction.

I swallow hard when I see a pair of black boots. Jerking my gaze up, I focus on Tiller, pretty sure my lips part and my heart is beating so hard that it will leave a bruise behind.

And then we're moving.

Piercing dark eyes are focused on me so intently that it's impossible to look away. They draw me in, our bodies getting closer as if he's a magnet and I'm iron shavings or some shit. Whatever the hell it is that's making me move, I'm happy not to question it. Especially when his gaze dips.

When I do the same, glancing at his mouth,

Tiller's tongue peeks out, and he wets his bottom lip. While I don't see it, I know there's a bar through it. Do I want to suck it and see what it feels like?

Damn straight, I do.

There's a moment that we pause. Maybe it's not apparent to anyone else but the two of us. But it's enough for our gazes to catch, for me to see how wide his pupils are blown, and enough for me to know that Tiller is as invested in this moment as I am.

# CHAPTER 2
## TILLER

LEON BRADFORD. I'M ABOUT TO KISS LEON "PULSE" Bradford.

My mind is screaming at me to pull away. This has trouble written all over it, but he's fucking sexy and has starred in my fantasies a time or two since the moment I saw his team photograph and watched some footage. I'd be a fool not to take the opportunity when it presents itself.

And holy shit, is he presenting himself.

The guy may as well have "Suck me... I'm curious" printed on a tee. I'm more than happy to make that happen, but first there's this kiss, and I intend to take complete advantage.

Our mouths connect, lips gliding, and fark me, the hitch in his breath is sexy. The sound pushes me on, and I unleash on him. If this is the only time I can get my mouth on his, I'm all in.

When his tongue brushes against mine, I snake my hand to the back of his head, cupping and keeping him close. Our mouths move in sync. There's no awkward false starts, no sloppiness. It's all simply perfect, but he's pulling away all too soon.

Once there's distance between us, my ears tune in to the hollers from our eclectic little group—most of whom I don't know. While I'm aware of the noise, the heavy pounding of my heart dulls their actual words. My gaze fixes on Leon. On his flushed cheeks. His moving chest.

And then he smirks, and it takes every inch of control I have not to launch at him and go for a second kiss. Easing away, I exhale deeply, trying to get my breathing under control. As I settle down, I quirk my lips at him and throw him a wink.

"Your turn." Leon's voice is unwavering as he looks away, his words sounding as confident as when I've watched him in postgame interviews.

Me? I'm wrecked. I feel unhinged. My heart is still hammering against my rib cage. Coming here was a huge mistake.

What the hell was I thinking?

Shit, I'm not even a student anymore. Nor have I ever been at this school.

Me returning home after traveling overseas and being bored is the reason I came to this college party like a sad fuck. Perhaps being here wasn't my brightest idea ever.

I clear my throat and am disappointed when Leon's gaze remains on the girl to his left, laughing and talking to her about something. I should be relieved. That would be the sensible thing, since the moment's vanished, but the clench and forming knot in my gut suggest otherwise.

"What the fuck?" At my side, Michael's words are barely a whisper, but they get my attention.

I peer over, and his wide eyes, filled with a touch of glee, stare back at me. Not knowing how else to react, I shrug. Since Michael's my cousin who knows me all too well, he's not buying my nonchalance.

"You're in so much shit." His chuckle is loud. He's far too pleased by my fuckup. But beneath that is concern.

"No idea what you mean," I whisper and turn away from him. As I do, my gaze snags Leon's. Curiosity is in his hazel eyes. They hold me captive before he darts a look at my cousin, then back to me before once more glancing away.

"Leon, man. What's going on here?"

Leon's cheeks heat, and he angles toward the

newcomer. It's Tyron Channing. Another star player on Brixham's champion basketball team.

"Dude, you playing spin the bottle?" Tyron's grin is wide and would be contagious if I wasn't more interested in Leon's response. His focus is entirely on his friend, and in his profile, I see the flick of a smirk.

"You know it." Lightness fills his tone. Gone is his reaction to our kiss. Before me sits Pulse. The man who's known for keeping his eye on the ball, the players, and having a special talent at reading plays before they happen.

"Huh." Tyron's attention turns to our group. I know we're a strange mix. His gaze lands on mine, and a squint forms. He's wondering if he knows me. I give him an up-nod before focusing on the abandoned bottle.

It's my cue to leave.

Three years ago, I left college. I really shouldn't be here.

"You ready to go?" I ask Michael, the sound of conversation starting again around us. "I'm heading out. You can stay, though, if you want." Since I'll be heading to my parents', it's not like I need a place to crash.

"Yeah, I'll head out with you."

I nod and stand, briefly looking around the group. I focus on Melanie, a senior. I know her because she's a local, so we went to the same high school—in different years, obviously. "Catch you later, Mel."

"You too, Tiller. Don't be a stranger now that you're back home."

I bob my head and smile.

After a quick round of goodbyes, I realize Leon's also standing, and he's moved to the side, next to Tyron. Our gazes meet, his searching, mine probably doing the same. All I know is that the kiss was hot, and if he doesn't regret it already, I expect he will soon enough.

I offer a small smile and take another step toward the door.

"Shit… you're Coach Maple's son, right? I thought I knew your face."

And there it is. With Tyron's words, I have no doubt the hit of regret is punching into Leon hard.

I turn back to Tyron. A meaty hand is being held in my direction. I shake the forward's palm, saying, "That's right. Tiller."

"Holy shit." Tyron pumps my hand. "Your hair, man… I didn't recognize you."

I don't explain that growing out my buzz cut was one of the first things I did when I left college. Gone was my short hair; for the most part, my longer strands were an easy enough distraction that College

Basketball Association fans didn't give me a second look. I was able to blend in with the faceless crowd, not wanting to be known as the number one draft pick who quit an hour before signing his contract to the League.

"I get that a lot." I shrug, super aware that Leon's gaze is on me.

"You sticking around, live locally now?" Tyron carries on, completely unaware of how hard it is to stay focused on him.

"I just got back from Indonesia a few weeks ago. I've been traveling for three years."

"No shit."

"Yeah." My laugh is quiet and a little more relaxed. "I'm hanging around for a while, though."

"You'll have to come to a few practices." He angles toward Leon, as do I. Leon is bug-eyed, and I'm sure he's close to panic. I wince, aware it was shitty of me, not only inviting him to play but also kissing him like there was no tomorrow, especially as I knew exactly who he was.

Fuck, what a wanky thing to do. I should regret it, but since I can still taste him, I'm not feeling as bad as I should.

"Leon, man, he should definitely come and check out a few practices, right?"

Leon nods a little woodenly. I don't add that my

dad's already asked me. Or even how just the thought of assisting has sparked my eagerness to return to the world of basketball. This time without the unwanted pressure or stress of playing pro.

"Hell, you guys play the same position." He smacks Leon on the back. "You should totally hit him up for some pointers."

Red spreads so quickly across Leon's face that I'm concerned. "Uhm… maybe," he settles on.

"No 'maybe' about it. Do you not know Tiller's CBA stats? He still holds at least three records."

This time I'm the one who I'm sure is bright red. It's been a long time since I've talked about my time in the CBA. Sure, Dad and I regularly chatted while I was away, and he also sent me his team's news and reels. We even talk strategy a lot, and I know he values my opinion.

"Don't sweat it. I'll set it up with Coach."

From Leon's double take and the forming horror on his face, I expect that means if it wasn't already arranged, Tyron would indeed make it happen.

Before we have time to respond, he clasps Leon on his shoulder. "Shit, I forgot we need to get to Sammy. It's the reason why I found you. Let's go, man." Tyron refocuses on me and shakes my hand again. "Tiller, it's good to meet you. I expect I'll be seeing you next week at training." The confidence in his voice makes it sound like it's a done deal.

And then he's stepping away, all but dragging Leon with him, but not before Leon's gaze snaps to mine one last time. I have just enough time to send him an apologetic smile before he's entirely out of the room, and I'm left with Michael, who's ushering me out of the house, muttering something about him making sure he watches this week's training sessions.

# CHAPTER 3
### LEON

"YOU MADE OUT WITH A GUY, JUST LIKE THAT?"

My shrug is too casual to be believable, but Kieran won't call me out. And his surprise? Well, it's understandable since, in the three years I've known the guy, he's only ever seen me hook up with women.

Plus, the whole kiss thing that happened at the party was almost as unexpected for me as it will be for any of my friends.

And how do they know? I told them. There's no way I could keep that shit to myself. What I didn't tell them was who it was with.

"Shit, I don't see you for a few hours, and I come home to this. How did I not see that go down?" He shakes his head, something like wonder and concern on his face. "You want to talk about it?"

The sound you hear is the stumbling of my heart. It's not quite panic, but the kiss with Tiller was unexpected and unprecedented.

Since Kieran's still staring wide-eyed at me, I huff out a breath. "I don't think so."

That expression on his face screams that he's not convinced. But the good friend and team captain he is, he doesn't push. "Okay." Uncertainty clouds that one word. "But if you change your mind, I'm here, okay?"

Relief at his response calms my racing pulse. "Yeah, thanks." I nod and focus on the wall clock in our kitchen. "Shit, I've got class in twenty. See you at practice." Even saying that word, my heart stumbles a little. You heard it, right? You also heard Ty saying he would talk to Coach about his son helping me out. Yeah, I didn't think I imagined it.

The thought of spending time with the man has my pulse going wild. But let's also go back to the huge, freaking gigantic elephant in the room. I made out with Tiller Maple. *Coach's son,* Tiller Maple. The same guy who was a hotshot basketball player and dropped off the face of the earth the day he was due to join the League.

I can't even wrap my head around it. I'm kinda pissed that I didn't recognize him, but Ty got it right. Tiller looks so different from the All-American basketball star I knew him as. Because of course I "knew" him; every basketball player does… or did.

I followed his games when in high school. Shit, it was one of the big pulls for attending Brixham, knowing his dad was the coach.

Grabbing my things, I get out of here, needing space from Kieran's worried stare, and step into the morning Georgia sun. As soon as the rays touch my face, I breathe a little easier.

The party was wild. Unexpected.

I can still taste Tiller's tongue, and when I really focus, there's the ghost of his touch on my skin. While I have no idea how we allowed our chaste kiss to get to that point—with my tongue in his mouth while enjoying how he gripped the back of my head —I don't regret it.

Not one single bit.

How can I when it was the sexiest kiss of my life?

I shiver at the memory. Goose bumps dance over my skin with the thought of his heat against mine. The scruff of his jaw—

And now I have a fucking hard-on… in public while walking to class.

Awkward much?

I readjust myself as discreetly as possible, which isn't easy when my junk's pressed against my zipper. Thank Christ for my laptop bag. Holding that in front of me while I sort myself out at least gives me a chance not to have the increasing number of students around me, zeroing in on my action.

Mission complete, I exhale and start thinking about my first class of the year. Or at least I need to attempt to. What I shouldn't think about is Tiller. Or how firm his grip was, or what his mouth felt like against mine.

And that steel bar? Hottest thing ever.

I smile and give an up-nod to a couple of people who call my name, completely distracted by the party. The last two days I spent the whole time obsessing, and honestly, I hoped I'd jacked him out of my system. The conversation with Kieran, though, has brought thoughts of Tiller front and center. I also wonder if Ty has already gotten word to Coach of his brilliant idea of Tiller attending practice.

Seriously, Ty is the one guy who manages to pull rabbits out of assholes. Yeah, I know that's not how it usually goes, but it does make it clear he's stubborn and the most persuasive person I know. He's a magician when it comes to getting the impossible done.

If he does start coming to practices—keep up; I'm back to obsessing over Tiller—maybe a repeat wouldn't be so bad. Exploring the chemistry would be an acceptable use of my time, right? And having the chance to blow my load would be a great way to unwind after a game or training.

Let's just ignore the fact that he's Coach's son. I don't want to spend much time thinking about that detail.

You're also wondering why I'm not freakin' the fuck out about hooking up with a guy, right? I've already sort of gone over this, so sorry for the repeat, but even though I'm downplaying it, it's exciting and kind of a big deal, right? Am I curious as hell? Sure. But it's more than that. And the instant spark between me and Tiller, the attraction that slammed into me… well, I'd be a fool to ignore it.

"Leon, wait up."

I pause immediately, recognizing Sammy's voice. "Hey," I greet when he reaches my side. "You sorted for all your classes?"

He bobs his head. "Yeah. Finally. I had to shift out of one class because of a clash with training, but Nelson over in admin got me fixed up. I need to head to the bookstore later. You wanna come with?"

"Sure. I ordered a couple of titles that are waiting for pickup."

Sammy snorts. "Dude, one of these times I'm going to get you to organize the shit out of me."

I shove him with my shoulder. "Hell no. Life's too

short for that level of chaos." He chuckles and doesn't disagree with me. "You got class now?"

"Yeah, room 238 with Macey."

"No shit. That's where I'm heading."

"Cool."

We head together to the lecture theater and find seats at the back. It doesn't take long for the rest of the students to file in and for Professor Macey to give his start-of-semester overview. Since I've had him for classes for the last couple of years, I know I can safely tune out for the first half of the session. It's not till the last thirty minutes that he'll go through the meat of the course and I'll need to pay attention.

"You heard anything about the new guys on the team yet?" Sammy whispers and leans in close.

I shake my head. "Not a single thing. You're asking the wrong guy."

Sammy pulls out his cell and shoots off a message. Since my phone vibrates in my pocket, I figure it's a group one. Discreetly, I tug it out and see the message he's directed at Ty.

Dancing dots appear before a message pops up.

> Ty: Of course. 1 sophomore transfer from Michigan U. 3 freshies. Banks is the kid to keep our eye on. Looks like he might have something about him. Gavin Jones screams cockhead. Davey... not sure yet.

I don't hold back my grin. Ty gets the scoop on everyone. That magician reference from earlier wasn't an exaggeration.

> Sammy: Where you at?

> Ty: Coffee and eating my weight in donuts.

> Sammy: Your ass is not going to thank you for it.

I grin and shake my head. Ty is a tank. Well, if a tank was a six-three basketball player with hands like huge-ass baseball mitts and shoulders so broad he has to turn to get through doorways. Only a slight exaggeration there.

Okay, beyond his height, the rest is pretty much bullshit. The "tank" thing is more about him being intimidating as fuck. I'm envious of the steel in his eyes, and he's perfected his "don't fucking think about it" attitude that has weaker players wanting to get out of his zone.

He's also pure muscle, so when he runs, it's a spectacular sight. I tend to get that "holy shit" moment when watching him, wondering how the hell a guy with so much solid muscle can run so damn fast.

> Ty: My ass is perfection. Since the gluteus maximus is the largest, most powerful muscle to work against gravity, I'd say my ass will be thanking me for the extra hit.

I snicker quietly, wondering if that's an actual fact or one of Ty's "facts." Honestly, the amount of shit that comes out of the guy's mouth, it's so hard to tell. Especially when each bit of random knowledge he imparts is shared with such conviction, I always have a moment of pause, unsure if I'm being a dumb shit or not.

> Kieran: Put down the donuts. Sammy, aren't you in class?

No way am I responding to any of the texts, not when Kieran's in dad mode. "You're in trouble," I whisper-sing to Sammy.

"Pussy," he says quietly out of the side of his mouth.

> Sammy: Leon kept harassing me about the team, making it impossible to focus, so I had to ask to settle him down. *sigh* It's a chore.

A glance toward the front of the room shows me that Macey's still talking away and isn't paying a lick of attention. That's my cue to flick Sammy's ear. Hard.

He barely disguises his "Fuck" with a cough. Meanwhile, I clamp down on my lips and try to get myself under control.

By the time class finishes, I've made sure I've followed the notes online and have a decent understanding of what's to come. For all I fuck around, I like to stay a step ahead. I suppose that's why I can get away with goofing off every once in a while. The extra preparation outside of class makes it worth it.

"You wanna head to the bookstore now, or do you have another class?"

"Now's good," Sammy says.

"You got your list?"

"In my email."

I bob my head, and we make our way around the library toward the south side of campus, where the bookstore is situated. It's not owned by the college and is just off the grounds. The store, Book Grind, also sells killer coffee.

"Did you hear that Tiller Maple was at the weekend's party?"

"Yeah." Like a dickbag, my throat catches, but Sammy's focusing on his phone, so I don't think he's paying that much attention. "I was with Ty, who recognized him."

And why I've held back the truth about Tiller being the guy I got a boner over? These fuckers, also known as my friends and teammates, are assholes. They'd never let me live it down and would rib me so damn hard. That's a headache I don't want.

"Cool, man. Ty said he's speaking to Coach, seeing if he can get his son to attend a few practices."

Already thinking that'll be awkward, I clamp my mouth shut. Not that I expect for one second Tiller would say anything. It's nothing like that. But I'm not exaggerating the number of hard-ons I've had over Tiller since kissing him.

Up close and sweaty with the guy on the court, I expect I'll find it difficult to run with a third fucking leg.

Thankfully, we arrive at the store, which cuts off further talk of Coach's hot son. I tug open the door, sighing at the welcoming scent of ground coffee beans.

"You want to grab us a table first?" I ask Sammy. "I seriously need to caffeinate."

"Sounds good."

He lopes off to claim us a table. There's still a few open. I imagine there's a lot of students still navigating the first day of school rather than seeking refuge in Book Grind.

Making my way toward the counter, I eye the pastries in the display. Spending my cash on crumbly, flaky goodness isn't the best idea, especially so early on in the school year. Over the summer, I worked my ass off to save enough to see me through as many days as possible. The less money I have to borrow, the better.

Looking away from temptation, I focus on the server. His back is to me as he bends to grab milk out of the fridge. Since I'm next in line, I wait patiently before the register, phone in hand so I can pay.

"Leon."

My breath catches, eyes widening when my gaze meets piercing brown eyes. "Tiller." Fuck, did that sound breathless to you? I sounded like an awestruck dick, right? Shit, is it too late to turn and run?

But then the handsome fucker smiles. He's all pearly white teeth, and the way his eyes crinkle, which I'm pretty sure means his smile is genuine, makes my heart stutter.

"You're here." I'm nothing if not observant. "Behind the counter." Yep, nothing gets past me.

Rather than scoff and call me a dumb fuck, Tiller tilts his head and slowly, oh so slowly, rakes his gaze over my body. How such a look gets me revved up is nothing short of impressive.

"That'll be because I work here."

Surprise mixes with confusion, and I dip my brows. While he obviously works here, since he's wearing a gray apron and is about to serve me, it begs the question of why. Why would Tiller Maple, the number one draft pick three years ago, work here?

# CHAPTER 4
## TILLER

THE WAY HIS THOUGHTS BOUNCE AROUND HIS FACE IS kinda sweet. Leon Bradford is easy to read, his emotions ripe for picking. I like that a little too much.

When he doesn't respond, I go easy on the man. It's only fair, since I sort of feel like I took advantage of him at the party. Not in a predatory, nonconsensual way or anything, but simply because I knew who he was.

Hell, I'm still blown away that he kissed a man. I also figured if he'd recognized me, no chance would he have kissed me.

And what a fucking delicious kiss it had been.

Not quite transcendent or anything as dramatic as that. But given a chance, I'm definitely up for more. The thought surprises me, even more so that I don't want to shy away from it. Apparently, me swearing off repeats three years back was bullshit.

Though technically, if we haven't screwed, is it a repeat yet?

"So, what's your poison, Leon Bradford?"

Wide-eyed, he stares back, apparently still confused by me being here. Either that or he's reliving our impressive kiss and is struggling to focus on anything. A guy can dream.

When he still doesn't answer, I smirk. "How about I take a guess?"

"Huh?"

"I'm usually good at figuring out what hot college guys' orders are." So maybe I'm not taking it so easy on him, but just look at the man. He's just begging to be flirted with. He's all olive skin, pouty-fucking-mouthed, with the sweetest hazel eyes I've ever seen. And then there's the floppy hair with curls that's the right side of adorable and the perfect length to grip hold of.

And don't get me started on the scruff on his face. Just imagining the feel of his cheeks on my thighs is enough to get me into all kinds of trouble.

"You think I'm hot?" Immediately, pink bleeds into his cheeks, and his eyes widen even further.

My lips twitch. "You are most definitely 'double-shot hazelnut cappuccino with extra foam' levels of hot."

"Holy shit."

A laugh bursts out of me. "Did I get it right?"

"Everything except the extra foam." With his words, he seems to remember where he is or maybe who he is. His shoulders relax, and he stands up a little straighter. A cute smile also tilts his lips. "You know my name."

I chuckle lightly, loving how his brain processes everything and slowly catches up. "Last year's champions. One of the most reliable guards any college team could ask for." Pink crawls up the column of his neck, something I like a lot. I continue, not wanting to stop our conversation and knowing the lull in customers won't last much longer. "Leon Bradford, excellent shooting guard and secondary playmaker." I quirk my brow, loving that I have his complete attention. "Sound about right?"

The pink has morphed to red in his cheeks, and I wonder how he'll respond… if I've pushed too hard.

After a beat, he licks his bottom lip, gaze roaming my face before he says, "Tiller Maple, arguably one of the most prolific and successful rebounders in college basketball in twenty years." He arches his brow at me, sucking me in so completely with his response that I rest my elbows on the counter, leaning forward.

"Averaged twenty points a game in his senior year. Was number one pick." Here he hesitates, and I understand why.

It made the sports headlines for a while after I caused a little bit of chaos and grief by pulling out of the draft at the last minute. Legit, I was the number one pick, but I didn't sign the contract, fleeing and disappearing instead. Yeah, I pissed off a few people that day, but it's not anything I want to get into right this second. My embarrassment hasn't quite faded.

Rather than continuing with a commentary about me bailing, he gives a barely there shrug. "Sound about right?"

I laugh, maybe a little too loudly, since I'm at work. It gets a few customers' attention, but I don't care.

Leon is unexpected. Interesting and cute. Talented and a whole lot gorgeous.

And from the back-and-forth, the extra fizz in my stomach can't help wondering, hoping even, that he's interested.

The ding of the door opening draws my attention, and a couple of customers enter. While I've only worked here for two weeks, I recognize that these are locals rather than just-returned students who will want coffee rather than books. It means I need to stop flirting and make coffee.

"I best get that coffee ordered. What did your friend want?"

"Oh, right, yeah, of course." He looks dazed, and that fizz in my stomach goes crazy that I'm the one who's made him dizzy. Something about my scintillating conversation or my mesmerizing brown eyes. Yep, I'm still fantasizing, so I'm just going with that interpretation. "He's simple."

My brow arches high.

Realizing what he's said, Leon snorts, his cheeks heating again. "Well, you didn't hear that from me, but I also mean his coffee order. Black coffee is great, and no sugar."

"On it," I say, going for broke and offering him a wink, really hoping there'll be a fresh flush of pink. And hallelujah, Leon doesn't disappoint.

I ring him up and tell him I'll bring his drinks over. After sorting the next order, I need to remain focused and make his coffees. Far too easily, my focus drifts to Leon.

He's sitting with Sammy, another Bears player. His teammate is chatting animatedly about something and pointing to his phone. Twice I manage to snag Leon's gaze; each time, my lips curl, and I receive a smile.

By the time I've gotten their order ready, I'm

almost bouncing with the need to speak to him again, get close enough that I can catch his scent.

I've no idea what it is about Leon that's captivated me. I still think my gut reaction of "bad idea" remains true, knowing that not only will Dad likely have something to say about me hitting on his playmaker, but there's a little voice in my heart that's prodding me and whispering something about learning my lesson. There's a flip side to that reaction that I'm struggling to ignore.

I want a repeat of that kiss.

I want to get to know Leon better. Find out what makes him laugh and discover how far his blush spreads down his chest. If there's a chance of tasting his cock, too, hell yes, I'm up for that.

I'm twenty-five and horny as fuck. I'm not the twenty-two-year-old who got played and felt forced into a future I didn't want before spectacularly disappearing without giving a shit how the cards would fall. I've also had a dry spell that I'm legit concerned about. Doesn't too much masturbation give you carpal tunnel or something? If that's the case, I'm more than ready for someone to help me.

And Leon Bradford may just be the man to help me scratch this itch that's refusing to be ignored.

# CHAPTER 5

## LEON

My classes whiz on by, and in no time at all, we're sitting around waiting for Coach. I spend a little time eyeing the new guys. Kieran's already welcomed them into the fold and done a general intro, so at least we know their names.

I just hope Ty isn't right about at least one of them being a prize dick. It's normal to take two or three weeks to gel with new members of the team, but having an asshole around makes that time drag on. We've been lucky the last couple of years, but when I was a freshman, we had a guy named Caleb join who was a show pony. Thank fuck he ended up tapping out, as he'd sent a shitty ripple through the team.

"You can thank me later."

I jerk at the sound of Ty's voice, realizing he's talking to me. "Huh?"

He grins and flicks his head in the general direction of the door.

I follow his line of sight, eyes springing wide when Coach enters, Tiller at his side. It's impossible not to react. I rake my gaze over his body, taking in his fit form, his tight black jeans with rips in the denim, and his chest-hugging band shirt.

He's hot as Hades, and by the time our stares connect, I know I'm screwed.

I want this man. Want to taste, explore, and find out more about him.

Sure, my dick is interested, but from the couple times we've met, the urge to get to know Tiller bubbles in my chest.

His smile is immediate and wide, and I like that it's directed at me. And then he's practically before us, his dad next to him, and I'm sure Coach is saying something, but my whole focus is on Tiller, on that cocky, self-assured smile that's kinda sweet.

An elbow in my ribs has me grunting. "The fuck?" I whisper and snap my gaze to Ty, who's staring at me like I have two heads.

"Coach," he hisses and angles his chin in the general direction of Tiller and his dad.

I jerk my focus to Coach, whose stare is hard and not even a little amused. Heat prickles my skin. "Sorry, Coach."

Narrowed eyes are set on me as he remains silent for one, then two beats. "Head out of your ass, Bradford. Or do you want time added before we even start?"

"You've got it, Coach. I'm concentrating." I don't dare switch my focus to Tiller.

"You know," Ty whispers at my side a moment later, once Coach has diverted his attention away from me, "almost anything can fit up your butt. Not sure about an actual head, but yeah, the butt's super flexible."

I slam my lips together, trying to ignore Ty's random oversharing of facts, and nod occasionally at what Coach is saying just in case he glances my way.

"Someone even lost a Buzz Lightyear action figure up their ass. Actually *lost* it," he continues, and it's impossible not to release a squeaking snort of a laugh before a look from Coach has me clamping down my reaction.

"Shh," I attempt, but Ty doesn't give a shit.

"I wonder if it was a toy fetish or a Buzz Lightyear fetish. I suppose Buzz is kinda alpha hot. That's a thing, right?"

It's no good. I side-eye him. "How the fuck would I know?" I whisper, shaking my head.

"You kissed a guy, right, so you must have thought he was hot. Was he *alpha* hot?"

"I don't even know what that means."

His nose scrunches. "I'll ask Kieran. Or maybe Dean. He looks like he'd know about alphas." He tilts his head to the side, stare intent. "You think he likes shoving things up his ass? I mean, other than dick? I wonder what that's like."

My mouth opens and closes. I have no idea how to respond or even if I should. That Ty's wondering about asses and anal shouldn't come as any surprise to me. But he also raises a valid question. Not about Dean or what he likes. Fuck no. I don't want to know what my captain's boyfriend is into. But the whole anal thing.

Hell, I have no idea if Dean bottoms. And fuck, I should so not be thinking about that. But color me curious.

It's best I turn to safer topics.

I wonder if Tiller is gay or bi or another interesting letter in the rainbow alphabet. While we kissed, and I'm pretty sure at the bookstore he flirted, that doesn't mean he's not straight, right? But if he's not straight, has he got experience with anal? Does he like giving or receiving, or does he like both?

I swallow hard at the latter. It's sexy… I think. I clear my throat, pointedly ignoring Ty while trying to will my dick not to respond to the idea of Tiller being vers. I like the idea a little too much, and my interest is well and truly piqued.

"Coach is calling you."

Ty's voice snaps my mind away from ass and dick, and I make a beeline for Coach, who's still standing with Tiller. Sweat breaks out on my neck, and my hands feel clammy. Somehow I focus on Coach as he tells me his plan for Tiller to spend some extra time with me. I nod in the right places, and I even manage a smile.

It's not until he pats me on the back and walks away that I wipe my palms on my shorts and make eye contact with Tiller.

His stare is intent. It dances around my face and settles on my mouth for a beat before reconnecting with my gaze. His focus entrances me, and the occasional peek of silver in his mouth is impossible to look away from.

"So, the old man wants me to show you a thing or two."

His words roll over me, and my mouth opens before I'm even sure what to say. *"Anal."* The word bursts past my lips far too loudly and so fucking unintended that I want to curl up and die.

Looking startled, Tiller stares, his brows touching his hairline. "Anal?"

I wince, my face on fire. What the fuckety fuck is

wrong with me? "Uhm...." But there's no save and no way I can pretend he misunderstood. "I... uhm...." I huff out a breath and glance away, my gaze snagging on the new guy Gavin Jones, who's openly staring at me, his face blank. A moment later, he's darting away with the ball, calling out to one of the other new guys.

In the next second, Tiller's in my space, so close I feel his warm breath caressing my lips.

"Were you thinking about *things* I could show you?"

Frozen before him, I can't even blink. All I know is we're so close that someone will be intervening at any moment. Like this, it's almost like we're going to throw down—if not that, then we'll start making out right here. I swallow hard, unable to step away like I know I should.

"Because I can," he continues, mercilessly darting his tongue out on his bottom lip and leaning his face so close to my ear that my whole body shakes. "That kiss was the hottest kiss I've ever had, and I'm more than happy to take things further. If you want?"

I'm nodding, the movement fast and on the edge of desperation.

And then Tiller is out of my space and a respectable three feet away from me, but his smile...

holy shit, his smile is incredible. It's broad and sweet and utterly focused on me.

It's only natural that a wide-ass grin splits my cheeks. How can it not when Tiller has flipped my world upside down, and I'm giddily hanging on for the ride?

# CHAPTER 6

## TILLER

My dick threatens to punch a hole in my jeans. I have no idea how I'll get through practice when all I want to do is grab Leon's hand and drag him away from here.

There's no chance I could get away with that, even though the image makes my cock throb.

Sitting on the sidelines, I watch Dad run the team's first practice, looking at how he likes to set things up. Sometimes I pull my attention away from Leon long enough to concentrate on the rest of the players. That only lasts a few minutes before I'm almost drooling over Leon's strong form, the way he's sure and confident. The way his training shorts hug his ass is an additional draw I have no issue admiring.

When he almost shouted the word *anal* at me, the

asshole I am simply leaned into his slip. Dropping the offer had been instinctive. That Leon had readily accepted blew my mind. No way would I question it, though.

My offer was genuine.

He's hot, which is a no-brainer. And then there's the kiss I can't shake the memory of. I just hope he's up for a good time and can keep this on the down-low.

I came out to my family the day before the first-round selections. Dad took it in stride, surprising me by hugging me and telling me he loved me. Yeah, my mind had been blown by that, since he wasn't a tactile man, let alone a dad who gave a lot of affection.

But me hooking up with one of his players would piss him off.

Like all coaches, he likes his players to be focused —their minds on the game and the win. Not necessarily single, though. He's not that much of an asshole. But me swooping in and causing a stir, he'd have something to say about.

I grudgingly accepted when he asked me to join a few practices. Not that I'm not keen to be here, but being a coach like my dad had been a dream forced out of me under the pressure of going pro. So yeah, I was nervous—still am a bit—at the possibility of finally chasing a career. When he'd asked me to spend some extra time with Leon earlier today, my acceptance had been a little too fast, too enthused. It was only my quick thinking by changing the subject and getting him to talk about the new players on the team that had stopped him from eyeballing me.

"Tiller."

Dad's voice cuts through me eyeing Leon just as he's doing some stretches that showcase his flexibility. I seek Dad out, spotting him next to Kieran, who I'm impressed by. The way he captained his team last year, all the way through to the win, was nothing short of remarkable.

I nod and make my way over, aware that my heavy black boots aren't ideal for this surface. I suppose I'll have to start dressing the part if I'm going to support Dad with some coaching.

"Kieran, meet Tiller."

I smile, reach out, and shake Kieran's hand. "Good to meet you, and congrats on the title. You played some impressive ball last season."

A wide smile breaks free on Kieran's handsome face. "Thanks, man. I can definitely offer you the same compliment. That game you played against Merryvale U was one of the best I've ever seen."

I know exactly which one he's talking about. It was one of the defining moments in my basketball career. The first time everyone believed I had what it took to go pro. It didn't seem to matter that just the thought of joining the League and having a future laid out before me I didn't truly want made me break into a sweat. "Thanks."

"While I want you to have focused time with Leon, I want you to work with Kieran and look at his plays to help consider Leon's role."

I nod as I listen to Dad. Kieran seems like a decent guy, so it won't be a hardship. "Can do," I agree.

Dad claps me on the back before walking away, leaving me alone with Kieran.

"I know practice is wrapping up soon," Kieran says, wiping trickling sweat from his brow, "but we tend to go and grab food after. You want to come with?"

"You sure I'm not going to mess things up, you know, being the coach's son? I don't want you to feel like you can't bitch about him for pushing you so hard 'cause I'm there," I offer with a smile. While I like the idea of getting to know the team better, I'm honest about not wanting to mess with their dynamics.

A large hand latches on to my shoulder, and I turn to see Tyron at my side, a wide smile on his face that I'm not used to. Usually when I watch footage, the man is the king of "don't mess with me" scowls. This smile is kind of unnerving.

"Nah, he's good, right, Key? He'll be able to give us the dirt on Coach." He removes his hand and looks at me, his eyes bright, gaze intense. "Plus, if you're going to whip Leon's ass into shape, you'll need all the help you can get."

He laughs while I smirk. I have no problem with spending hours working, worshipping… whatever… Leon's ass. Though I'm not sure how any of these guys would feel about that.

"Yeah, sure. I can always eat," I say, referring to food and not Leon's ass. Though the possibility of the latter is something I'm down for too. Joining the team should give me time to get to know Leon better. But I'm beginning to seriously rethink my living situation and staying at my parents' place. In fairness, when I moved back, the last thing on my mind was hooking up and having the privacy to do that.

I wonder who Leon lives with.

"Excellent." Kieran nods in approval, his attention moving behind me. A new smile appears on his face, brightening his eyes and making him appear even more handsome. I angle to see who's responsible for this sort of reaction.

A girl's sitting on the bench. Her head's buried in a book, so I carry on searching, only pausing when

Kieran moves past me, jogging over to a guy who's tiny compared to Kieran's height and muscle mass.

He surprises the hell out of me when he scoops the guy into his arms, tugs him close, and plants a smoldering kiss on him.

Huh. How'd I miss this development? Sure, I haven't been back in the country long, but is Kieran Kendall with a man?

"That's our boy Dean." Tyron's deep voice is harder than before when he spoke to me. I drag my attention to him and take in his stare. It doesn't matter that I'm older than him or that I have a couple of inches on him. That look is intimidating as fuck, and I'm not a guy who backs down quickly. "He's also the team's mascot."

I snort out a bewildered laugh. "No shit." When his gaze narrows, I lift my hands, placating. "I don't mean anything by that. Just…" I search for the words. "…pleasantly surprised is all."

His intense stare doesn't waver, and while I'm aware of Leon joining his side, I don't look away. "Why? Because he's a gay basketball player?"

"Well, yeah. It's great that he's out and clearly has the team's support." Honestly, it's fucking awesome and something I'd never felt able to do.

"He does," Tyron pushes, gaze still flinty. "He has Coach's support too."

Leon shuffles at Tyron's side, and I make eye contact. He's looking a little unnerved by Tyron's stiff shoulders. I offer him a smile before refocusing on Tyron. "Well, Dad would hardly be an asshole about someone's sexuality, since I'm gay as fuck and he has my back."

The shift in Tyron is immediate. His shoulders loosen and lose their rigidity. His smile is striking too. Jesus. I roam his face, appreciating his smile while wondering why there are so many hot players on the team.

A slight cough immediately halts my perusal, and I focus on Leon. That he's quirking his brow at me is adorable. I'm more than happy to reassure him that while Tyron is an attractive guy, Leon has my complete attention. And honestly, with how he's captured it, it will be a struggle to move on if I get another taste.

My grin is wide and solely for Leon. "I'm joining you for dinner. Something about me owning your ass."

Leon's quirked brow shifts into two raised ones while Tyron laughs loudly, clapping his hand on my shoulder again. When Leon's gaze narrows on the movement, my stomach flips, hands tingling to reach out to him so I can finally press my lips to his.

# CHAPTER 7
## LEON

Any minute now, I'm going to lose my shit and hide Ty's secret stash of candy bars, maybe even throw them all away. When the fuck did he get so handsy with someone he doesn't know? He's the absolute epitome of reserved and grumpy. Usually. But if he presses his shoulder against Tiller's or smiles that widely again... yeah, that candy stash is history.

I take another bite of my pizza, narrowing my gaze at Ty and how he's monopolizing Tiller. Sure, I know I'm being a sulky asshole, but none of my friends know he's the guy I kissed, and they definitely don't know that since Tiller made me an offer I don't want to refuse, my dick's been hard enough to pound nails.

But I also get why Ty's not the only one hanging

on to Tiller's every word. The man is mesmerizing. He's also funny as fuck and has experiences I can only dream about.

"And that was in Indonesia?" Ty asks with a laugh.

"Bali," Tiller confirms, his gaze flashing to mine for a second. His lips curl, making my heart speed up before Ty's loud mouth recaptures his attention.

"You know, Indonesia has the hottest spot for the Ring of Fire," Ty says. "Ring of Fire," he repeats, tilting his head, a twinkle appearing in his eye. "You think that means there's flaming assholes everywhere from spicy food?"

I sigh none too quietly. "Seriously, Ty." I shake my head, holding back my amusement as I behave like a jealous fuckhead and refuse to let him know I find him funny.

"What?" Ty furrows his brow, but that twinkle doesn't disappear. Since the man is a legitimate genius, we all know he's winding us up.

"The *Pacific* Ring of Fire," Tiller intervenes, not knowing Ty's mindboggling IQ. "Yeah, something to do with the earthquake belt, right?"

The way Ty stares at him makes me uneasy. "You knew that?" He's almost panting, and I need to find a way to stake my claim. Yes, it sounds ridiculous. As far as I'm aware, Ty is not interested, but since my dick's fascinated by Tiller, it's crystal clear that I am.

"Yeah." Tiller chuckles, the sound washing over me. My ire grows like the green-eyed fucker I am, wishing I caused that laughter.

Jesus, I seriously need to pull my head out of my ass.

"So," I say quickly, dropping the uneaten pizza slice on my plate, "Tiller, when do you want to hook up—" I freeze but can't pull my gaze away from Tiller's brown eyes. "To sort the training sessions, I mean. You want to work through times now? We can head back to your—"

The shake of his head cuts me off, and the slight blush touching his cheeks has me curious. "Uhm... I actually moved back home with the 'rents since returning to the States."

He's embarrassed, which is surprisingly endearing. A smile tugs my lips. "That's okay. We can head back to our place."

"Yeah, totally," Ty says, enthusiasm loud and clear in his voice. "I wanna know more about Indonesia. I'm sure you've got a shitload more facts—"

"Ty," I say quickly. "Maybe another time, yeah? Coach wanted me to get things locked down with Tiller."

Ty stills, his gaze assessing, and I work hard not to blush or look at Tiller. For all his grumpy, loud-mouthed ways, Ty is worryingly perceptive. After a beat, he nods, eyes locked on mine. "No problem. It can wait."

I swallow and exhale slowly. "Okay. Are you guys heading back now or…?"

Studying me far too hard for my liking, Ty twists his mouth. "Not yet. I need to talk to Key about a few things."

"You do?" Confusion colors Kieran's words.

"Yup," Ty answers, not looking away from me. "We'll be back in an hour." Then the fucker lifts a brow and his lips twitch.

He knows. As I said, he's ridiculously perceptive, but he does a good job at destroying my frustration. It looks like his candy stash will remain safe for another day.

"Yeah, okay," I rush to say. Focusing on Tiller, who's wearing a bemused expression, I stand. "You good to go now?"

"Sure," he says and gets out of his seat. "Good to meet you guys." He peers around the table. "I might see you back at the house later, maybe."

With that, we leave the pizza place. My hands tremble, and my heart's going wild, and with every step we take away from my friends in the direction of home, I find it harder and harder not to grab hold of Tiller and push him against the wall, eager for another taste.

Since he remains silent at my side, I expect, or at least hope, he's feeling the same tension, the same need. Just another couple of minutes and I'll be able to tackle him, tug him to my room. Once the door's locked, I'll be eager to see if he'll make good on his words.

I should probably be more nervous than I am. Honestly, I'm too curious and horny to question it, let alone doubt my attraction.

Finally we arrive at my shared house. I tug out my keys and open the door, inviting Tiller in with a small smile. When I close the door, I ask, "Do you want a—" But my words are abruptly cut off as his palms latch on to my arms, and he backs me against the closed front door.

A whoosh of air flows out of me. Wide-eyed, I take him in.

Tiller's all dark-eyed intensity as his gaze flickers around my face, capturing my stare before he focuses on my mouth.

"Or you can just kiss me." The words fall freely from my mouth, startling me with their depth and gruffness. That I barely know the guy is irrelevant. Fuck that. I'm a twenty-two-year-old senior, and this right here is my time to explore, drop my inhibitions, and take what I want.

And right now, I want Tiller Maple.

"I can definitely do that," he murmurs as he leans into my space, his lips so close that the warmth of his breath makes me tingle.

Unable to stand waiting for a second longer, I clasp his waist with one hand and place the other on his jaw. The fact that his breath catches is all levels of hot, knowing he's as affected as I am.

His lips meet mine with sweet urgency. I all but wrap myself around him, wanting his body close as our mouths move with just a hint of exploring tongue. But it's when he groans that I know if I don't move now, my housemates will find out before I'm ready that I'm beyond horny for this man.

"Bedroom," I gasp against his lips.

He nods, our mouths still connected as he slips his palm under my tee, his skin warm against my back. It takes every ounce of self-control I have to walk him backward, eyes briefly opening to navigate my movements.

Tiller continues to unravel me, his kisses moving to my neck. I'm a shaky mess of desire in his arms, but at least I can see so we don't fall on our asses. If we fall, we'll go at it right here in the communal space.

"Fuck," I groan when he sucks my flesh. I don't even care if he leaves a mark. Hell, from the way my cock throbs, it's clear I like the idea a little too much. "Stairs. Now." I force myself to pull away, scrambling to find his hand. I clasp it and tug him up the staircase, a desperate moan escaping when he palms my ass.

Fuck yeah. No one's ever been close to my ass before. Sure, there's been pats and slaps over the years, but like this—a squeeze, a caress—never before. I'm so on board to explore and take everything Tiller is willing to give me.

We stumble into my room, me turning toward him so I can close and lock the door. "We have less than an hour," I manage to say as Tiller claws at my T-shirt, tearing it off me.

His heated gaze connects with mine. "I can work with that," he murmurs, the sound seductive and full of promise.

"Yeah?"

"Oh yeah," he says, tugging on my bottom lip before stepping away and unbuttoning his tight jeans that right now leave nothing to the imagination.

I swallow hard as I watch him undress, transfixed by the expanse of skin he's revealing. And holy fucking hotness, his ink spreads from his arms to his chest, down his sides to his hips. The patterns are intricate and encompass a selection of delicate designs that I definitely want to explore.

"Fuck, you're so sexy." The words escape me with a gruffness I've never used before.

"That right?" Tiller pulls off his jeans and stands before me, completely naked. "That the first time you've said that to a guy?"

I nod, unable to tear my gaze away from his twitching dick and the silver ring attached to the end of his cock. My breath rushes out of me as my eyes widen. "I don't know if I should wince or do a happy dance."

His chuckle is enough to draw my attention away from his glistening cock. Maybe I should be more embarrassed about my words, but I don't have it in me in the face of his quirked brow and sultry smile. "It hurt a little, having it done," Tiller clarifies, "but it was totally worth it."

Glancing down at the ring as he speaks, I swallow before swiping my bottom lip with my tongue. "It was?" My voice is only a fraction above a whisper as I'm mesmerized by his piercing.

A new level of gruffness dips his words low. "Fuck yes, it was worth it. The sensitivity is insane." He lifts his hand and traces his thumb over my wet lip before nudging my chin up so my focus returns to him. "Not only for me," he says pointedly.

There's a brief pause before he says, "I have to ask, do I need to use a condom?"

His question pulls me up short, and don't I feel like an idiot. I've never had sex without a condom. But a bj? Fuck, I so have been sucked off without disclosing I'm negative.

Admittedly, I've never gone down on a guy before, but that's something I should know to ask, right?

"You can if you want to. Use a condom, I mean, but you don't need to… health wise," I tag on awkwardly. I roll my eyes, at myself more than anything. "I mean, I'm negative."

His smile is sweet, gaze still all heat and desire.

"Me too. I'd never put you at risk."

The uptick in my pulse at his words has me swallowing hard.

"This all okay, then?"

His question draws my brows low as I struggle to catch up to what he previously said before I zeroed in on his silver ring. He's making sure I'm okay. While I don't see any worry in his expression, he's definitely curious. I also like how he's checking and ensuring I'm still in this. "Definitely."

My answer pulls an immediate smile to his kissable lips. "Good." Releasing my chin, Tiller unbuttons my jeans. "Whether this is your first time or your hundredth," he says, unzipping me and tugging the denim and my boxers down my hips, "it's fine with me." With an unwavering gaze, he lowers to the floor as he eases down my jeans. The sight has my breath hitching. "Just know if you change your mind —" He indicates for me to step out of the material. I do so immediately, my breaths escaping in short, shallow pants. "—that's okay too."

I don't have time to form a response. I can't. The wet heat of his mouth covering my dick makes it impossible to do anything but latch on to his head and fall into the feeling of him sucking me off.

For the love of an epic bj... hell, I've had more head than I can count since being at college, but this, right here... the way Tiller hollows his cheeks and takes me so deep I see stars, everything becomes crystal clear.

Bi all the fucking way.

If this is what a man can do, what Tiller can do, why in the ever-loving fuck didn't I figure this out sooner?

I want to laugh and cry and thrust into his mouth while begging him to keep doing this to me forever, but my balls tingle, and as much as I want to come, I want to do other things with Tiller.

"I'm gonna...." I attempt to ease away, but Tiller's having none of it.

He latches firmly on to my ass, gripping and squeezing, and when the fucker eases a finger against my crease, the pad pressing against my opening, it's not stars that I see when I explode down his throat.

Fuck no. It's a whole motherfucking galaxy.

I'm shooting into the sky and spilling my load. And I'm pretty sure my groan is so loud that my throat will be hoarse tomorrow.

"Fuck," I gasp as he pulls off me, making me shudder when he licks the end of my dick. I'm so sensitive, I think my cock's gone numb. "I didn't want to come yet." I peer down at Tiller, my eyes still slightly crossed and my legs shaky.

Brown eyes filled with smoldering glee peer up at me. Tiller looks thoroughly impressed with himself. Rightly so. I've never come so hard. I tell him as much, and he chuckles, kissing my quivering thigh as he stands up.

"I think you've got at least one more in you," he says, leaning in for a kiss. I dive right in, holding on tight and sucking his tongue into my mouth.

I don't want to let go, but this is apparently the Tiller show, and he's leading me to my unmade bed before he eases me backward, my thighs hitting the mattress. Our mouths part as my ass makes contact, Tiller's impressive dick right next to my face.

My mouth waters, and I wonder what he tastes

like. Not only that, if I try to give him head, will I gag and turn him off? Will I even be any good at it?

When Tiller reaches for his dick and holds the root, he leans forward and paints his precum against my lips. "You want to taste that first before you try something else?" The husk in his voice is so incredibly hot, but as much as I want to see his face, I can't pull my attention away from his dick. Or the glinting piece of silver.

"Yeah," I say, licking my lips and committing his taste to memory.

"Fuck," he groans, dragging my attention to his face. With his bottom lip clamped between his teeth, Tiller looks debauched. His lips are red and puffy, and a spark in his eyes makes me feel bold.

"You think you have one more in you too?" I ask, encouraged by the way he's staring at me.

His nod is immediate, lighting me up and making me smile.

"So if I do this…" I lap at his dick, enjoying the salty tang, my tongue exploring the ring. "…and you come down my throat…" I lick a line along his cock. "…well, after that, we can both come together?"

"Fuck yes."

Tiller worked up is a thing of beauty, and I'm desperate to see what expression he has when he comes. "Okay then."

Despite my shaky exhale, I want this. So what if I gag? In the past, it's been kinda hot when a girl's gagged on my mouthful. As for knowing if I'm any good or not? Fuck it. There's only one way to find out.

Running my tongue over his hard length, I take my time exploring the softness of his skin that contrasts so perfectly with the steel underneath. It's the vein that gets my attention, though. Sure, I have my own, but to feel the thrum under my tongue is different. Exciting. So much so, my dick stirs valiantly, perking up with interest.

I trace my tongue around the end, paying attention to the metal before dipping into the slit, once more tasting. His flavor is different from mine. Any guy who says they haven't licked their cum is full of shit. We're too horny and curious not to have a little sample.

Tiller's groan and the tightening of his glute under my hand catch my attention. I glance up and watch his stomach muscles tauten. My pleasure is immediate, loving his reaction before I open wider, take him fully into my mouth, and suck like my life depends on it.

"Leon. Fuck."

I double down, enjoying the way he gasped my name. But I need to see his face, his reaction. Peering up, I capture his gaze. Half-lidded, lust-filled eyes stare back at me as, once again, he clamps onto his bottom lip.

"Suck me harder," he says between moans, his eyes never wavering.

I'm more than happy to oblige. I'm totally nailing this, right? I grip the base of his cock to help with the friction, attempt to regulate my breathing, and inhale through my nose before taking him deep, until his cock hits the back of my throat.

I gag immediately, pulling away. But fuck no, I'm not giving up. And from the depth of want in Tiller's eyes, he has no issues with my gag reflex. Hell, I expect he'll be more than happy to offer himself up as the man to practice with.

Unfazed, I lick, lap, and suck him, my hand still working his root.

"That's it." He jerks his hips, thrusting into my mouth, something I've always held back from doing. And holy shit, I like it. Love his hard thrusts. Love the way he's struggling for control.

I readjust my rhythm to keep tempo, encouraging him to fuck my mouth. He does so with increasingly fast, shallow strokes, not going deep enough to make me gag. One day maybe my throat will be able to handle it. My dick throbs at the thought, fully hard and ready for round two.

"I'm gonna come."

Our gazes catch, and I know he's giving me a warning. Spit, swallow, or pull away and jerk him off? Fuck, the sexy dilemma is a hard one. Pun absolutely intended.

I hesitate for the barest of seconds. Fuck it. I'm in this now.

That I like dick is now a given. And I'm determined to drink his cum and love the taste of it too.

Keeping eye contact, I make my intentions clear by not pulling away. His slow, soft smile is worth it. The heat I see in his gaze, the way I know I'm the center of Tiller's thoughts, is heady and spurs me on. I continue to suck and attempt to caress the underside of his cock with my tongue. But it's when I cup his balls and tug and squeeze, which has his hips jerking and legs shaking, that he finally stills and the first taste of his release fills my mouth.

Yeah, this right here is definitely where it's at.

# CHAPTER 8
## TILLER

The blow job is sloppy and messy—and perfect. Leon sucking me in was one thing. But swallowing me down, which is now crystal clear to me that he's never done before, is quite possibly the hottest thing I've ever seen, let alone experienced.

My legs shake as he pulls away and rubs a hand over his mouth. His eyes are watery, lips puffy, and I absolutely know this time we have together isn't going to be enough.

"You okay?" I ask, my breathing heavy.

"Yeah," he croaks, the sound drawing a smile from me.

"Good." I nod and angle over him, encouraging him to lie back. "You wanna scoot up the bed?"

With a bob of his head, he does just that. The whole time I hover over him, not ready to move out of his space. When he's eased back, I settle my weight on him. Leon's groan is immediate, as is my own when I realize how hard he is again.

There's a flash of something in his eyes when I trail my fingers down his neck, but I don't freeze. So far, Leon's been forthcoming about what's going on in his mind. I believe if something has changed, if he wants to stop, he'll tell me.

When the pads of my fingers graze his hip, he shudders, eyes closing and staying that way for a few seconds. He really is beautiful. Certainly prettier than most of the other guys I've been with. But when you add in his strong shoulders and toned game-fit body, there's nothing feminine about the guy.

"So, you want to try something else before our time's up?"

"Yes," he says immediately, eyes springing open. His eagerness is something special, something I could easily become addicted to. "What's the time?" There's a hint of desperation in his voice, and I'm impressed his brain's clear enough that he has it in him to check.

"My phone's all the way over there." I indicate toward my jeans by the door, quirking my lips. "I'm kinda comfortable right now."

He chuckles, his hip moving with the action,

tugging fresh moans from us at the friction. "I've got this."

I'm about to complain that I don't want either of us to leave this position just yet, but when he looks over at the bedside table and I spot an iPad, I smile. I grab it, my movements a little cumbersome as I flash the pad his way. His eyes widen.

"Let me have that. Ty's sent me a text."

I hand it over as he checks and use his distraction to nuzzle his neck, trying to commit his scent to memory. I think the mixture of sweat, body wash, and Leon could quickly become one I could get familiar with. Lapping at his neck, I sigh, content, only to freeze at Leon's "Fuck."

Pulling back, I peer down at him. "Something wrong?"

"My housemates are on their way back. Ty texted five minutes ago. I didn't hear the alert."

"Shit, okay." I pull away and stand, hesitating before reaching for my jeans. "Uhm, so, I kinda figure this is new for you."

Leon pauses in his scramble for clothes, his gaze connecting with mine. "Yeah." He winces. "But it's not like I have a problem with, uh… that you're a guy. I just would like to figure things out first." A grimace appears. "Is that shitty of me?"

I shake my head immediately and step his way.

"You working stuff out needs to be done in your own time, and actually"—I rub the back of my head, feeling guilty about what I'm about to admit—"if anything, I'm the one who'd appreciate this staying on the down-low. My dad...." I trail off, not quite sure how to continue.

"Fuck." Wide-eyed, Leon nods. "Shit, yeah. Not sure how Coach will react to this." He bobs his head again. "I get it," he adds before surprising me by asking, "But if I do tell my friends about me, uhm... do you need me to keep your name out of it?" A blush spreads across his cheeks, and there's no way I can deny him such a request.

"That's okay. As long as it doesn't get back to my dad." Unable to resist, I reach out and stroke his jaw. "Yet." I swallow, feeling uncomfortable putting myself out there like this.

The one word earns me a huge-ass smile. "'Yet,' huh? So does that mean you want to do this again?"

"Absolutely. Plus, I really am happy to help you with the game." I don't add that I would like the chance to get to know Leon better. What I've discovered already, I like a lot. Maybe it's ridiculous that the thought of spending more time with him makes my pulse race, especially considering our different situations. Still, I learned years ago to embrace experiences that get my blood pumping.

Leon Bradford offers that in spades.

"Yeah, okay. Uhm… yes to all of that." That Leon leans into me and makes a move to kiss me shouldn't make me as happy as it does. But a guy initiating a connection like this gets me revved up. Not ideal, since we need to get our asses moving, but with his lips pressed against mine, I reciprocate. Our tongues brush across each other's for the briefest of touches, lips moving slowly before Leon uses the head on his shoulders and eases away. "You want a beer, and we'll chat downstairs?"

"Yeah, sounds good," I agree, taking a step away and focusing on dressing.

We've been in the kitchen for a minute, my beer just placed in front of me, when the front door unlocks and a chorus of loud voices and multiple conversations rumble into the house. Tyron's loud "We're back" catches my attention, though.

"In the kitchen," Leon calls with a smirk, gaze flicking to mine. Perhaps seeing the question in my eyes, he whispers quickly, "I kinda think Ty suspects."

My brows pop high. "Seriously?" How he'd know anything is beyond me. Over pizza, I'd spent most of the time talking to Tyron rather than Leon, for a start, despite how much my attention wanted to gravitate to him. There'd been a moment there when

I thought Tyron had been flirting, but a few touches from an enthusiastic speaker didn't necessarily mean he was coming on to me. Not that the man wasn't good-looking, but he was too intense for me.

The group of guys enters the room, Tyron leading the way. From the way his gaze darts to Leon, then at me, I think Leon's right. He certainly knows something.

"So, this dickhead has the patience of an impatient sea cucumber." Tyron gestures toward Sammy, the handsome small forward with startling eyes.

He pauses in the doorway, frowning and staring at Tyron like he's lost his mind. "An impatient what?"

"Don't—" Kieran starts.

"Sea cucumber," Tyron says with a roll of his eyes.

"—ask," Kieran finishes with a heavy sigh.

"Is that even a thing?" Sammy asks, ignoring his captain.

Kieran's doing this whole "abort" thing with his hands and pretty impressive facial expressions, while Tyron's face turns incredulous as he says, "Of course it's a thing."

"Huh," Sammy says. "But how's it impatient?"

Tyron seems stumped for a moment, his mouth opening and closing before his gaze narrows. "Impatient is part of its name, and it wouldn't be called that if it wasn't impatient." He tugs out his phone, his focus intent.

"Sammy, really?" Standing to head into the kitchen area, it's the first time Leon's spoken since his housemates entered the room, and the slight roughness to his voice gets my attention immediately. It's hard to hold back my smirk and my dick twinge, knowing exactly why his voice sounds so scratchy. I have no idea whether Leon sees my movement or senses me, but his attention snaps in my direction. His blush is so swift, I have no doubt my lust is clear as day on my face.

I try to pull it back, knowing he wants time to figure things out, so I quickly look away. With Tyron's focus still on his phone and Sammy seeming to realize what everyone's reaction is about, I exhale.

"Yeah, yeah, okay. I know better," Sammy grumbles, throwing down his bag and walking more fully into the kitchen. "Did you guys figure out training?" He looks at Leon, then at me. "Ty was being weird and tried to lock us all down with some shit or other. You know what he's like. Anyone would think he didn't want us to come back in case we were crashing something." He chuckles, sticking his head in the refrigerator.

It's a good thing, too, as Leon sort of freezes. His lack of response is enough to have Kieran and his boyfriend eyeing him. It also has Tyron dragging his head away from his phone.

"Sammy, the only thing you'll be crashing is your ability to do a lap around the court if you spray that cheese into your mouth. That's seriously gross." Tyron's response effectively draws everyone's attention away from Leon, as we all stare at Sammy squirting yellow crap into his mouth.

Don't get me wrong, I've eaten my fair share of unhealthy food—even fake food like that—in my time, but it's that he's following up with pickles and a bag of M&M's that's grossing me out.

Leon's staring in horror as he says, "Dude, you're acting like you're pregnant."

Sammy pauses his chewing, glances around at us, and then simply shrugs. "Whatever. You've just got no imagination."

Bentley, the Bears' shooting guard, dumps his bag next to Sammy's. "Not sure it's lack of imagination that's the problem here."

Sammy rolls his eyes at his friend, carrying his post-pizza feast to the table.

"Were your college housemates like this?" Leon asks. He hurries away from Sammy and takes the seat right next to me. The other guys mill around the room, breaking into a different conversation.

I snort, thinking back to my time at college.

"Pretty much. I think I had a friend equivalent to each of yours." My stomach tightens. It's impossible not to think about that time without a blast of frustration. At least now the emotion isn't crippling. Traveling, escaping, and a lot of reflection have made it easier to smile and focus on the good times. It also gave me the tools to finally return home.

"Yeah?" Leon sounds a little cautious. My gaze locks on his, wondering if he could hear the slight shift in my tone, or maybe he saw how my muscles contracted a little.

"Definitely." I smile, giving myself a mental shakedown. "You meet a whole bunch of characters here, right?"

He bobs his head, his attention unwavering as he half turns in his seat to look at me more fully. "That's the truth. Are you still in touch with any of them?"

"Yeah, most of my team. Barry and Coleman especially. We chat a couple of times a month. They both met up with me when I was traveling as well."

"Cool. That must have been good." A smirk appears on his lips that have lost some of their puffiness. "So you're saying I've got no chance of escaping this bunch of losers next year when I finish school, huh?"

A chorus of "Fuck offs" and "As if you don't want to see mes" erupts around the room. I chuckle—their interactions, their complete affection for each other, are not at all surprising.

"You see," Leon says pointedly, blowing a kiss to Bentley when he flicks a potato chip at his head, "there's no chance of escape." His voice is full of fondness, which I can relate to. "Anyhow, schedules. What's yours look like?"

I tug out my phone. "Book Grind schedules out two weeks in advance."

"And you're sure you're okay giving up extra time to go over plays?"

"Absolutely. I have a heap of free time at the moment. Plus, Dad asked." When Leon's eyes dim, I add quickly, "But even if he didn't, I'd like to spend time with… uhm… to help you up your game and prepare you for the season."

I don't look around, too chickenshit to in case my slip got on anyone's radar. And from the tender look Leon's directing my way, it's clear he heard it. That smile right there lets me know he liked hearing it too.

"You work at the bookstore?" Bentley asks, cutting through the silent exchange I've been having with Leon.

"Yeah," I answer, "but as a barista."

A confused frown appears on Bentley's face. "But, like, why? You were the number one draft pick, right?"

"Bentley," Leon says quickly, shooting him a look that I'm sure is meant to be "shut the fuck up." "You've got a chip stuck in your teeth," he says pointedly, effectively shutting him up.

While I'm not surprised Bentley asked, since I figured most of them would be curious, discomfort settles in my chest. It isn't the great big secret or drama that I know the media at the time made it out to be, but that doesn't mean I want to share my humiliation of a kid running scared.

"Listen, I'm going to head out." When I stand, Leon furrows his brow but stands with me.

"Yeah, sure," he says a little uncertainly. "You want to text me your schedule, and we'll get something sorted?"

My shoulders relax that he's okay with my clear need to escape. "Yeah, sounds good. Here." I pass him my phone. "Send yourself a text so I have your number."

A sweet smile chases away the worried pinch on his face as he accepts my phone and shoots off a message. "Done."

I take my phone back and glance around the room. "Good meeting everyone. I'll be seeing you all soon."

They say goodbye as I'm heading out, ready to

make my way back to the campus where my car is still parked.

Once we're alone and at the front door, Leon steps closer, some of the concern from earlier returning to his gaze. "I'm sorry about Bentley. He's usually more sensitive than that."

Immediately I shake my head and reach for him, giving him a gentle squeeze at the waist before letting go. "Don't worry about it." When Leon doesn't appear convinced, I add, "Honestly." A quick glance around tells me we're still alone, and I lean in for the briefest of kisses.

It's barely a touch, but I feel his heat fiercely, and the moment lingers somehow.

That appears to do the trick. Well, his concern is gone, but a flash of heat peers back at me.

Can he feel this too? The spark? The connection?

I'm likely to be getting way ahead of myself here, but it's been so long since I've felt a pull so purely. And for the first time since being gutted by my ex-boyfriend three years ago, I want to learn more about this man rather than run at the possibility.

# CHAPTER 9
## LEON

As soon as I return to the kitchen area, Ty's focus zeroes in on me. He's not doing a great job of keeping his attention low-key, but I try my hardest to avoid eye contact and instead pick up my unfinished beer.

Rather than settling at the table with Ty, I fetch a glass to pour some water, Sammy still feeding his face next to the sink.

"Tiller seems like a good guy," he says, thankfully after swallowing a mouthful of food.

"Yeah, seems to be." I clear my throat and ignore Ty's movement.

"I think having his input will give us an edge," Sammy continues, oblivious to the sweat that's broken out on the back of my neck as Ty stands and heads toward us.

"Uh-huh," I respond, focused on Ty while trying to not actively look.

"You think he left because I mentioned the draft?" Bentley says from a few feet away.

Hearing the discomfort in Bentley's voice, I look at him fully. He's frowning, his gaze on me. "I don't know, but I wouldn't sweat it. He doesn't seem like the kind of guy to get mad or pissed off, especially at a harmless question." That's not to say I'm not curious.

Tiller pulling out of the draft had hit the headlines and was all the sporting world could talk about for a time there. He'd fallen off the face of the earth, or apparently disappeared traveling. While his dad was still active in the CBA and had an excellent rep as a coach, I'd never seen or read one interview with him talking about his son either.

It's something I've never thought about before, and I suppose it's a little strange how it all played out. But I expect Tiller had his reasons. I'm interested to know what they were, even though, based on his reaction, I have no intention of asking, or at least not anytime soon.

"I'll ask around," Ty says, stepping into our space to get into the conversation.

I frown. "About what?"

"About Tiller and what happened to him."

I shake my head, immediately uncomfortable. "Fuck no. It's none of your business or anyone's."

"It's weird, though, right?" Sammy says, not helping the situation.

"Yes, that. Who knows what he was into. Maybe he was actually kicked out or something." Ty folds his arms, and I'm a little worried about the glint in his eyes.

"I said no." My voice turns hard, enough that the conversation around the table stops. It's rare I get anyone's attention this way. I'm usually the one to go with the flow and not cause waves, but this whole conversation isn't okay. "I mean it, Ty. You need to let this go and trust Coach and trust me that he's a good guy and that whatever happened is no one's business, okay?"

Remaining quiet, Ty studies me, his shoulders rigid. I sigh at the stubbornness written all over his face. He gets this way sometimes and becomes immovable in his ferocity, but I can't have him messing with Tiller. Ty has some serious trust issues and other peculiarities—his obsession with "facts" being just one of them. But he's also extremely protective of those he cares about.

Finally, he speaks. "Can I talk to you alone?"

I sigh but nod. If he's going to push this thing

with Tiller, I'd prefer for it to be in private anyway. "Sure."

"My room," he says, and I'm relieved, as I'm sure my room smells of sex and cum.

As we walk out, we have the attention of all the guys. There's a mixture of concern and interest, maybe a little surprise too. I shoot a quick eye roll to Kieran, attempting to downplay this, but I'm not sure it works as his apprehensive gaze follows our movements.

Once we're in Ty's weirdly tidy room—though, to be fair, we've only been back a few days—he shuts the door, and I sit down on the chair at his desk.

"You don't need to answer," he starts, "and if you don't, I won't be pissed, but is the reason you're being so defensive because you're hooking up with Tiller?"

And there he goes, proving just how astute he can be.

I consider my answer, my thoughts bouncing around in my brain while my emotions do the same in my chest. I settle on "I'm not pissed, but I think Tiller's past has nothing to do with you or anyone." When his lips purse, I know I'm going to have to be extra clear about this, even if it upsets him, 'cause yeah, despite his hardass attitude, Ty is the biggest softie I know. "That you're so focused on invading someone's privacy surprises me... disappoints me." I hold back my wince, seeing my words hit the mark.

Pink spreads quickly across his cheeks, and then he blanches. I give him a moment to work through his thoughts, his reaction. Finally, he sighs, sitting heavily on his bed. "I'm sorry. I'll let it go. You know it's only because I don't want you hurt, right?"

My heart softens. Ty is a good guy, despite being a pushy asshole at times.

"I know." He's spent years dealing with people being pricks, so he lives on the defensive. "I know you go into protective mode, but you don't need to here."

After a beat of studying me, he relents and bobs his head. "Okay." He worries his lip, and it's clear he's waiting for more.

With my heart hammering, I admit, "Tiller's the guy I kissed at the party."

His eyes widen in surprise. "No shit."

I snort. "Yeah, no shit."

"And tonight?"

I clear my throat before saying, "Yeah, we kinda hooked up."

Ty's grin is instant, and so big that I laugh. He's the one guy I open up easily to. Maybe it's his upbringing that makes him so good at listening and getting people to spill their guts. Whatever it is, I'm grateful I have him to share this with.

Perhaps it'll help me work things out.

"Fuck yeah," he says. "Was it hot?"

I nod, heat pressing down on me in memory.

"And you like him? You're planning to see him again? Outside of training, I mean?"

"Yeah. He says he wants to. I'd like to get to know him." I purse my lips, grimacing a little about how to articulate my next words without sounding like a prize doofus. "I liked it a lot. More than with any girl."

Rather than responding immediately, he takes his time, gaze on me, that big brain of his no doubt mulling things over. "You know you don't have to put a label on anything, right? If you want to, you can, but you don't have to."

"Yeah. I just think it may help me understand my reactions better. Like, I've fucked around with plenty of girls. Enjoyed getting off but haven't *loved* it. Saying that, bjs have always been better than outright fucking."

The truth of my words settles over me. Not only that, the thought of fucking Tiller or him me spreads fresh heat through me. It's something I'm keen to explore.

"I've noticed guys before," I admit, paying attention to Ty's brows shooting high, "but I don't know. I've never really felt the pull or been actively looking, you know?"

"Yeah, I get that."

His words have me pausing. "You do? Have you...?" I can't help but think about his reaction to Tiller over pizza. Fuck, if he's interested in Tiller.... I hold my breath, waiting.

"Thought about it a time or two. Even more so recently."

Wow. Okay then. I think Ty's rendered me speechless. Yet I don't know why I'm so surprised, considering I'm a walking example of being completely clueless while navigating this chasm of self-discovery.

Realizing I'm legit just staring at him, I shake myself. "Okay... uhm...." A snort laugh escapes me. "This is kind of unreal, right? Like, I know everyone's different and attraction can be fluid, and there's no 'one size fits all,' but I suppose my only real knowledge is from Kieran." I shrug, feeling like a dope saying this to Ty, of all people. "He's known forever he's gay."

Growing up in a spit of a town out west meant I was pretty sheltered. There were certainly no out kids at school. Thank fuck for my parents, who, despite my pretty insular experiences in town, ensured I had an open, accepting view of the world.

"So have you, uhm, met someone you like?" Ty hasn't dated at all since I've known him. Last year he was focused on a girl for a while, but nothing came of it.

"Not really."

That's not a no, right? Or is that just me over-thinking it? My thoughts immediately flit to Tiller. Fuck it. If I can't ask Ty, one of the most open-minded people I know, one who's honest to boot, then I'm screwed. "So you're not interested in Tiller?"

You see that curl of his lips right there? Yeah, that's the one. He's amused and finds me especially entertaining. "Aw, you don't need to worry about me trying to make a move on your man."

"He's not—"

"Don't even bother denying it."

"One hookup does not make him mine."

"We'll see."

I roll my eyes. "Fuck, you're annoying."

He bounces his brows, but an alert on his phone distracts him. He tugs it out of his pocket and scans over it. Ty's brow creases, his frustration evident.

"Okay?" I ask.

With a heavy sigh, he flicks his gaze to me. "Just my sister being a pain in the ass."

I can only imagine. His twin's at this college and likes to party a little too hard. She's pretty much the bane of Ty's existence.

"I need to call her," he says.

That's my cue, but first… "Can you keep this quiet?"

"Of course." His answer is immediate. "You know I've got your back."

I nod, confident he speaks the truth. "Thanks, and please don't start poking around in Tiller's past."

For a solid five seconds, he stares at me without saying anything. Now, that may not seem very long, but have I mentioned how freaking intense my friend is? Just wait till you get to know him better. It's hardly a surprise so many people find him intimidating. Finally, he bobs his head. "I won't."

The good thing about Ty is that I believe him. He's not one for lies or bullshit. Sure, he spouts random facts and sometimes "facts" that boggle my mind, but Ty is someone I trust implicitly.

"Thanks."

I stand and leave him to whatever drama his sister's got herself into. We're only in the first week back, which doesn't bode well for how his year will go.

Rather than heading to the kitchen, where I can hear conversation, I go to my room. The scent of sex hits me. I'm hella glad I didn't bring Ty here. The smell makes my dick twinge, though, wishing we'd had the chance to go for the second round. At least Tiller indicated he wants to see me again, and I'm more than okay with that.

The man has completely caught my attention.

I spot my cell on the floor, where it fell earlier in my haste to undress and get my mouth on Tiller. I swipe it up and smile at the two new notifications.

One is when I messaged myself from Tiller's phone; the other is from Tiller.

I add his name to my contacts, then roam over his message, my smile immediate.

> Tiller: I was thinking a date tomorrow night. You available?

Surprise slams into me, my racing heart swiftly following, right alongside a big-ass smile.

A date? Hell, I can't actually remember the last time I went on one. Shit, was it high school? I worry my lips, racking my brain for a memory of my last date. All I can recall are hookups at parties, mostly with a faceless girl dropping to her knees.

I know, I know, that makes me sound like a complete player and a bit (maybe a lot) of a dick-head, but I'm not, I swear. Okay, perhaps I am a little. But I wasn't lying earlier when I mentioned hooking up had always been about the end goal of getting off, and a mouth has been the only guarantee of that. The more I think about it, the more pissed I am with myself, having never really thought about why the very idea of sex hasn't gotten me completely revved up.

Until now.

I swear I didn't think I was this dim. Apparently, I know nothing.

Yep, a total Jon Snow moment right here.

> Me: Yeah. I have workouts but will be finished by 7.

I stare hard at my screen, willing his response to come through, feeling a little giddy that I've agreed to an actual date with Tiller. Bouncing dots appear, and I hold my breath.

> Tiller: I'm closing up the bookstore tomorrow. Will be done by 7:30. Meet me there?

> Me: Sounds good. See you then.

I toss my phone onto the mattress and lie flat on my back, staring at the off-white ceiling. The excitement in my stomach isn't going to calm anytime soon, and that's okay. Beyond basketball, especially last season's big win, I can't remember when I was this eager for anything.

I like it a lot.

---

I SPENT EXTRA TIME IN FRONT OF THE MIRROR STYLING my hair before heading to the bookstore. All I can say is thank god for Ty. He ran interference when my friends hassled me about where I was going and who I was making myself look good for. I'm not ready to tell them anything yet. Maybe if it was a regular dude I'm meeting up with, I would, but this is Tiller Maple.

There's nothing remotely regular about the man.

While I'll handle the ribbing, I don't want to get on Coach's shit list. And some of my teammates have loud mouths—louder than Ty's, which is a feat. The difference is Ty doesn't spill secrets. Ever.

At the shop entrance, I take a deep breath. Tiller's putting up chairs after wiping down tables. He's focused, the concentration on his face evident in the few lights still on.

I tap on the locked door, and his gaze snaps my way, his smile wide and immediate. In a few steps, he's at the door, unbolting it and letting me in.

"Hey," he greets, surprising me by leaning in and

kissing my cheek. Before I can respond, he flicks the bolt, which is great as it allows me to center myself. I've never been this worked up or invested in a date before. Rather than freak about it, I welcome the slight discomfort, willing it to shift into excitement, maybe a bit of nervous expectation.

"Hey," I finally say, his focus once more on me while taking me in. "You had a good shift?"

"It was okay." A small smile follows his words. "I'm just about done here."

"I don't mind you putting me to work."

A broader grin appears at my offer. "In that case, I'll wipe over these last few tables if you can stack the chairs after."

We work together clearing up, Tiller sharing with me stories about his day, me telling him about my degree and this semester's classes.

"You didn't want to study at Brixham U?" I ask out of interest as Tiller empties the dishwasher.

"Hell no." A chuckle spills out of him, making me smile. "Dad is an excellent coach, but he's also a drill sergeant. He would have come down twice as hard on me." The shudder is exaggerated. "Plus, this is where I grew up, my high school not far away. I wanted to leave home, get out and explore the world."

"Well, it sounds like you did that. Did you spend all your time overseas in Indonesia?"

Tiller closes the dishwasher door and shakes his head at me. "That's everything. You ready?"

"Definitely."

He bobs his head and leads me out before locking up after him. Once outside in the darkening evening, we walk side by side to the parking lot. I walked here, so I figure we're taking his car wherever we go.

"I was in Indonesia for six months," he says, drawing us back to my question. "Before that, I spent time in Thailand, Japan, about a year or so in Europe."

"Wow. And you what, just took an extended vacation or something?" I don't think his family is that well off, but what do I know?

"No. Worked in bars and coffee shops, most of it off the books as I didn't have the right visa. Worked in a fish market for about a month in France. It's put me off fish for life."

I laugh and scrunch my nose. "I bet. When I was in high school, I worked on a pig farm. Put me off pork for at least a couple of years."

He bobs his head and side-eyes me. "Do you work during the summers too?"

"Yeah. I grab as many hours as possible at the supermarket, as I can do night shifts. During the day,

I usually get hours at the diner my mom works at. Mainly in the back, flipping burgers or doing dishes."

I'm not going to lie. I wait expectantly for his reaction. While I have no idea what his mom does for a living, his dad's a big deal in the CBA. Already that's a world apart from my parents.

My dad works as an engineer in a local pharmaceutical factory. The same place he's worked since he left school. They've never lived anywhere else, and I'm the first kid in the family to attend college.

"Sounds like good, honest work," he says, stopping at a silver car. "We do what we have to, right?" His gaze holds mine, and I can't help but take a step closer into his space. The parking lot is empty. There are a few streetlamps in the area, casting shadows as dusk draws in.

When my sneaker nudges his boot, he tilts his head. I also hear him swallow. "Talking about *doing* things." My lips twitch, but I'm hoping he also sees the need in my eyes.

"Yeah?" The one word is laced with amusement, and he quirks a brow.

"Where are you taking me on this date?" It would have been so easy to go down the route my dirty brain wanted to, but despite my chubbing cock, I want to learn more about Tiller.

Chuckling, he reaches out and places a hand on my waist. A welcome heat spreads through me. "There's an open mic night at a bar I know. It's usually pretty quiet as it's midweek, but they also do great burgers."

Interesting. I've never been to an open mic night before. Music's good and all, but since basketball dominates my life, it doesn't leave much room for anything else. "Sounds good."

He bobs his head, kisses my cheek once again, which has my pulse speeding up something ridiculous, then opens the door for me.

I don't know what to say. I'm equally charmed and a little embarrassed, but I just go with it and take a seat, pointedly looking away rather than at him when he closes the door.

A moment later, he gets in, and I don't even need to look to know he's smirking. Just to check, I take a peek and narrow my gaze. "Something funny?" I challenge with no real conviction, pretty sure I know what he finds amusing.

"Nope." He pops the *p* before winking at me. "It's been a long time since I took a cute guy on a date. I think I'm going to love it."

"Asshole," I mutter, fully aware my face is the color of a tomato. "And I'm pretty sure I'm ruggedly handsome."

"Uh-huh, because that difference is so important to your masculinity?"

I roll my eyes, my lips twitching at him calling me out so successfully.

"If it makes you feel better, you can call me pretty." A weird fluttering eyelash thing follows.

I snort out a laugh. "You are kinda pretty."

"Yeah." He nods, apparently delighted. "I can totally make pretty work."

"Your ink helps," I find myself saying, casting a glance his way as he starts driving.

"You like my tattoos, huh? Thought I saw some appreciation in your eyes yesterday."

A flash of heat hits my stomach, quickly shooting to my balls and stirring my cock to life once more. I shift a little uncomfortably. Maybe we should just head back to my place, but all the guys are there. There's only so much interference Ty can run before everyone gets suspicious.

"You doing all right over there?" Tiller's brows quirk high as he side-eyes me with a knowing smile.

"No," I tease, unwilling to admit my embarrassment of being so easy to read. Instead, I'm going to own this and turn the tables around. "I need a helping hand if we're going to make it through the night."

The swerve of the car has my eyes widening

before I snap my attention to Tiller. He's white-knuckling the steering wheel, his gaze darting to me.

Thoroughly pleased with myself, my dick hardens even more, and I grin. "Or mouth. I'm easy."

"Fuck." His gaze travels to my groin, and like the asshole I am, I press my palm against my dick, grunting a little at the contact.

"Are *you* doing okay there?" Amusement colors my words, despite the desire pulsing in the car.

Tiller's jaw locks, which is a new level of sexy. He also speeds up before putting his blinker on. I peer out the window rather than feeling him up like I want to. He seems too tightly wound up to handle that distraction.

We're on the outskirts of town, and he's pulling into a street I don't know. It doesn't seem to be residential. A few buildings come into view, and it's clear they're industrial, all with parking lots, most dimly lit.

Heat unfurls in my stomach. "You planning on doing something in particular out here?" When he doesn't respond but grips the wheel even tighter, I drop my focus to his lap. He's wearing deliciously tight black jeans again, and I'm sure if his cock is as hard as mine is, he's uncomfortable.

The nice guy I am, it's best I do something about that, especially as we're no longer on the main road.

I reach out, pop his button, and unzip him. The sound of his gasp accompanies the movement. While it's getting dark, nighttime's not yet settled in, and there's enough light to have me widening my eyes.

"You're commando," I grate. I almost swallow my tongue, but it has much better uses. "Shit. You're turning me into a dick whore." I barely notice his startled laugh as I unbuckle, turn, and tug him out.

His laughter stops immediately.

"Shit, wait, let me pull over."

Waiting is the last thing I want. His dick is right here, fucking weeping for attention. So I do what any decent guy would do: I shove my hand into his lap and latch on, pulling him into my mouth and sucking like he's my favorite damn lollipop.

I'm going to town, bobbing up and down, head knocking against the steering wheel, but I like this too much to care about my discomfort. I love the taste of him… get off on how his whole body is so taut, he might combust.

"Back seat." I hear the words but shrug him off. Seriously, I'm like a man possessed. It feels like I've been waiting my whole life for this, for his taste, for how right the weight of a dick on my tongue feels.

"Leon." The word is a gasp as he fumbles for his belt.

At his movement, I have no choice but to detach. I

do so with a whine I've never made before. But I don't give a shit. How can I when a need so visceral threatens to make me explode?

Yes, we had yesterday, but today feels different somehow. More. Maybe it's that we're on an actual date. Maybe I'm not as terrified of having a dick in my mouth. But something inside me has snapped.

Though I'm far from broken.

This right here, with Tiller, finally makes sense.

*I* make sense.

A rough palm finds my jaw, pulling my gaze.

"Leon, you with me?"

After meeting his eyes, I nod before closing my own and breathing heavily. His concern catches my breath, and while a trickle of mortification is beating away in my chest, I refuse to let it win.

"Do you want to stop?"

Immediately I open my eyes. "No."

A tender smile drifts onto his lips. "We can do whatever you want," he says. "I can guarantee that whatever you want, I'll want just as much." He waits for my acknowledgment before he continues, "You want to tell me what just happened?"

I stare at him, willing myself to own what's happening. Own my reaction. In many ways, it's easier that we don't know each other that well, that there's so much more to learn. It also helps that I'm crazy attracted to him. "It feels right, being with a guy," I admit, adding, "with you."

His lazy gaze roams my face. It seems like he can read all my thoughts and emotions. "I like what we're doing," he starts. "I'm also enjoying hanging out and getting to know you better." He runs his thumb over my bottom lip, his eyes following the movement. "It's been a long time since I've considered getting to know someone."

"As in dating, right?" Feeling a little more centered, I quirk my brow. This here is a lot of real talk, especially since I can still taste his precum and his dick's still out of his jeans.

Do I feel like a douche for saying it, even though I'm aiming for levity despite really wanting him to say yes? Maybe just a little. But that click... that rightness that's settled in my gut in my frenzy of getting my mouth on him is more than me wanting dick. Specifically, it's Tiller's I want. *His* I want to explore. The man I'm getting to know is the only reason for my interest and excitement.

"Yeah." His voice softens, and I get the sense that he's a little overwhelmed by the pace of all this. "As in dating."

You see this grin right here, the one on my face? Yep, I look unhinged, but since Tiller's matches, I don't give a shit.

# CHAPTER 10
### TILLER

How is it that I'm totally gone for this guy?

My dick's out, a little cool with Leon's drying saliva, but the only thing that feels exposed is this vulnerability dancing between us as we talk about dating.

The wide, open smile he shoots me, though, settles my pulse.

"Dating sounds like something I'd like to try... with you."

Any panic has already been squashed with what I'm sure to god is honesty between us. His expression is too raw, voice too sincere for it not to be.

"Me too," I offer, not even surprised at this point.

Closing myself off for three years hasn't been much of a hardship. Or it didn't feel like it at the time. Truth is, one-night stands start to feel empty.

Whatever void the connections were filling quickly dissipated by the time my release cooled.

And now there's Leon.

Young, talented, and so fucking eager. But it's how candid he's being, talking this shit out like he left college years ago, rather than being the senior he is.

I like him for it. Want to know more about him. I want to discover what makes him tick. What makes him laugh and smile. Hell, what even makes him sad so I can try my hardest to keep misery far away from him.

"So, starting our date in the back seat…." A smirk and a raised brow are directed at me, but it's the heat in Leon's eyes that has me catching up.

"Fuck yeah."

I press my mouth to his before hauling ass out my car, tugging the driver seat forward, then scrambling into the back seat. By the time my ass is on the cool leather and I'm tugging down my jeans, Leon is scrabbling to follow, his laughter loud in the otherwise quiet night.

"Warn a guy," he says with a snicker, his gaze greedily doing a lap of my body.

"You just need to pick up your game." It's so easy to tease Leon, have this comfortable banter. "Be ready to move and react."

Leon snorts but wastes no time in tugging down his jeans. As he does so, I haul off my tee. Fully naked in the back seat should feel surreal. But all I feel right now is horny, and so desperate for him.

Will this be difficult to bullshit our way out of if a patrol car pulls up beside us? Absolutely. That's not going to stop me from taking what I need.

And right now, I need his mouth on mine, and I have to feel his skin against my body.

Leon's head's not fully out of his T-shirt before I grip him and tug him to settle on my lap. Fuck. A groan tears out of us.

His warm chest presses against mine, his ass planted firmly on my thighs, and it would be so damn easy to get him to ride my fingers before he rides my cock. But not now. Not like this.

The first time I bury my cock in him, I want him spread out and crying out for me. I want to worship him, taste every inch of skin, trail my tongue over every crevasse, get him to ride my tongue.

I angle up, tugging his face, desperate for anything we can share in this moment.

A kiss, a slide, a parting of lips, and a fierce moan spills out of me.

"Fuck," I gasp before my mouth slams once more against his.

The tight grip of his fingers in my hair has my

hips jerking. I'm desperate for friction, eager to feel his cock pulsing in my grasp.

I glide my hand over his erection that's trapped between us. On contact, Leon moans and angles away, giving me more room. Grinning down at me, he's all desire and heat.

He shifts back even more, and I reach down, moving my cock so it presses against his. When I glance back up into Leon's hazel eyes, there's a wild desperation that wasn't there before.

"You want me to jack us both off?"

"Fuck yeah." He bobs his head, a tremble in his tone that makes my balls draw up high. "Give me your hand." Desire flares in his eyes, and fuck if it doesn't smolder when he licks a long line on my palm.

"Jesus." My breathing hollows out.

Satisfaction fills his gaze, and when I wrap my hand around our dicks, my fingers nowhere near close to fully circling their combined girths, Leon gasps and drops his forehead to my shoulder. "That feels so fucking amazing."

It does, and I haven't even done anything yet.

I move my hand, my palm sliding over us. The tightness isn't great and the friction isn't all that, but my need spikes. This is Leon's cock pressed to mine, and that's hotter than any other hand job I've ever given or received.

Leon angles back, and I know his gaze is on our dicks. I don't stop moving, luxuriating in the warmth of his skin, committing to memory how his breath hitches.

I nudge his chin, needing his lips. Pressing his face close to mine, Leon captures my mouth. I breathe him in and continue stroking. When he moans, he tears his mouth away. Before I can grumble about the loss, his hand snakes between us and wraps around our cocks, his fingers sliding over mine.

"Jesus. I need to come." Desperation coats his words.

He's not holding back, letting me see his need, feel his desire. It's a gift, one that's heady and sends goose bumps dancing across my skin.

I work us faster, tighten my grip just a fraction. But it's enough.

Hips jerking, he grunts, moaning a "Holy fuck, yes."

Our gazes connect just as his lips part.

Sparks, bright and blissful, shoot up my spine. Leon tenses as warm, wet cum spills over our hands. That's all it takes for my body to become rigid, and my release spurts out of me.

"Holy…." It's all I can manage. I can't close my

eyes, too busy soaking in the sight of our combined cum.

My cock jerks in our hands, and I groan. Leon's matching groan makes me smirk.

"That's…," he pants. He shakes his head, and I meet his gaze. Looking thoroughly blissed out and fucked, Leon is a thing of beauty.

*Holy shit.*

I still when he releases our cocks. But rather than also releasing my hand, he lifts it between us and doesn't stop until my hand is next to his mouth.

My eyes spring open wide as he darts out his tongue and swipes a long line up my finger.

My spent cock jerks valiantly, and at his groan, my lids droop as a fresh ripple of desire works its way up my spine.

"Now that—" He draws my cum-coated finger into his mouth and sucks it lightly, releasing it with a pop. "—is so fucking delicious."

He looks so fucking self-satisfied and lust drunk, my brain short-circuits.

There's only one thing I can do. Grinning widely, I shake my head, mesmerized by the man above me. As I pull him toward me, making my intention clear, I whisper, "Fuck, Leon, I think I'm going to like dating you a hell of a lot," before claiming his mouth.

# CHAPTER 11
## LEON

Practice this morning is brutal. But it's also ridiculously fun.

That may suggest I have a sadistic streak, but I swear I don't.

Instead, the sweat pouring off me, much like I've been submerged in a vat of the stuff, makes me smile. Hard.

The reason why?

Well, that may have something to do with me tugging up my training jersey whenever Tiller is close by. Of course, this is only to wipe my face and has nothing to do with the way Tiller's gaze gobbles me up. And that I've seen him back away a couple of times and hold his clipboard in front of his sweat-pants? Heck, that's one mighty fun bonus.

And totally worth my sore, tired muscles.

"Leon."

At the sound of Coach calling me, I race over to him. He's been talking to Jones, who, as soon as I'm standing before them, clenches his jaw and backs away.

"Yeah, Coach?" I ask, not even a little fazed by Jones's animosity.

He's been an asshole since day one, near enough. So much so that I'm both over it and used to it. I'm also able to easily ignore him.

"I want Tiller to be running drills with you."

"Okay, Coach." With the loud pounding in my ears, I can barely hear my words.

"He's got my notes on creating driving opportunities," Coach Maple says, briefly making eye contact before frowning at whatever Jones is doing. I follow his gaze.

The fuck is he doing?

The rookie takes being a dickhead to a whole new level. He also seems to have a death wish considering the way he's smirking at his cell rather than running drills.

"Jones," Coach hollers, and I take that as my cue to move my ass. Not that it's not fun to see a dickwad like Jones being reamed by Coach, but me hanging around and gawking will just get me roasted.

I head toward Tiller, not even having to look

around to see where he is. Whenever we're in the same room together, I'm viscerally aware of his location. It's a hell of a good thing I can multitask.

"Where do you want me, Coach?" Somehow I keep my voice steady and innuendo free. No small feat. Not when he's wearing a Bears coaching jersey and sweatpants that hug his ass to perfection when he bends.

Tiller quirks his brow at "Coach," but while he's not officially a coach, every time he attends practice, which is a lot, he's right there front and center, running drills and sorting out our tired asses like a skilled pro. "Shot fake and one-dribble pull-ups first."

I bob my head. Spending time with Tiller is always awesome, but getting his undivided attention has my pulse pounding that little bit harder.

"I'll act as guard if you want to get in triple-threat position," he clarifies. "I've been watching some of last season's footage."

"You have, huh?" I like that a lot. I'm tempted to ask if he liked what he saw, but I'm trying to stay professional, remember. It's best I file it away and tease him about it later.

The man has an impressive stoic expression. It's close to rivaling Ty's.

I hold back the twitch of my lips. Sure, I want to

tease and flirt, but I also want to impress the fuck out of him.

"We need to work on shooting on the move, knowing when to make the right pass, take the right shot, and when to fake it."

He's right. Decision-making is always tricky. When my heart's pumping, the pounding of feet loud, reading the opposition while trying to get in my teammates' heads is paramount.

"Remember, this is all about trying to create scoring opportunities," he says, getting into position as my screen.

And then it's on.

He pushes me—not physically—challenges me.

By the time I have no choice but to wipe the sweat out of my eyes—for real this time—Tiller's smiling at me so big that I pause.

We're close. So close I can feel the heat of his skin.

Dipping my voice low, I ask, "What's that smile for?"

"You." His gaze roams my face. "You're one hell of a playmaker, Leon."

Receiving his praise is something I could get used to. I want to bask in it, step closer and get all up in his business. Instead, I say, "That means a lot. Thanks." He goes to move away, but when I tell him, "You make one hell of a coach," he pauses.

An expression crosses his face that I can't quite decipher. A gentle smile follows. "Thanks, Leon. That means a lot too."

I'm not quite sure what it is that's happening here, but it's something. I just wish I could find out.

He edges back again, and I exhale, knowing this is not the time or place. That doesn't stop me from saying, "You have a shift tonight, right?"

Tiller nods. "Till eight."

"Can I see you?"

The call of my name has me turning and giving Kieran an up-nod. But I can't go until I have Tiller's answer. We hadn't made plans to see each other tonight. Between studying, training, and his work schedule, it's been tricky, but I can't not take the opportunity to spend more time with the man.

He's getting under my skin.

My gaze returns to Tiller. The slightest smirk kicks up his lips.

"Yeah. Meet me at the end of my shift."

There's no holding back my happy-as-hell smirk. And even as I jog away, my limbs aching, my sweat drying, and I'm sure I stink something fierce, Tiller just keeps giving me reason to smile.

"What's with the deranged smirk on your face?" Kieran stares at me like I have two heads.

"What?" I roll my eyes at him, but not even that dims the happy glow in my chest.

Nor does his narrowed gaze as he assesses me.

"Shit, man, did you hear Coach lay into Jones?" Sammy appears at Kieran's side, something close to glee on his face.

A heavy sigh slips from Kieran. "What's he done now?"

Sammy shrugs as I say, "He was on his phone rather than running drills."

"Jesus." Kieran runs a hand over his face.

"Gather around." Coach Mulligan indicates for us to get our asses into gear.

We do so immediately, even Jones, who's got a face of thunder.

Once we're settled, Coach lets us know tomorrow's practice is an hour earlier. None of us dare groan. He also reminds us of the upcoming charity car wash we're organizing, as part of our community hours we're expected to put in.

By the time he's finished, we haul ass. Most of us have lectures at nine this morning, so it doesn't give us much time to shower off and inhale some calories before making it to class.

I'm showered, dressed, and just tying up my laces when Jones throws his training kit to the floor.

I arch a brow in his direction, wondering what his problem is, just as he glances over his shoulder.

"The fuck you looking at, Bradford?"

Confusion slams into me. "The hell you pissed at me for?" Not that I especially care, but the dude seriously is a jerk. The sooner he's off the team, the better. I just hope that happens before our first game of the season.

Huh, perhaps I'm not as unaffected by his bullshit as I thought.

"Perhaps if you weren't getting special treatment from Coach's degenerate waster of a son, we'd all be getting a fair chance at starting line."

My confusion morphs into anger. The fuck did he call Tiller?

I spin so quickly, my gaze just for him, it takes me a beat to realize Kieran's stepped in.

"You've got a problem with how Coach does things, you go to him. If you can't handle that, you come to me." Kieran's tone is the tightest I've heard in a long time. While he's the epitome of together, that doesn't make him a pushover. Something Jones has never seen.

My body is vibrating with the need to tell Jones to go fuck himself, but I hold myself back.

"Rather than trying to stir things up and look for

blame elsewhere, you need to look at exactly what you are and aren't doing in practice."

The whole locker room is still, silent beyond Kieran's words of steel.

"You want to be on this team and get Coach to recognize he didn't make a mistake bringing you in, get your head out of your ass, off your phone, and lose the attitude."

Still glowering, Jones doesn't speak. His jaw tightens, and for one small moment, I seriously think he's going to be a dick and attempt to slug Kieran. If he does, it'll be the last time he's in this locker room, and with the way Ty's body's locked up a couple of steps away, I can't imagine if he is foolish enough to take a swing, it'll find its mark.

"You hear me?" Kieran pushes.

Jones's jaw's still rigid, but he sensibly nods before he turns, grabs his bag, and storms out of the room.

There's a hiss of air around the group, numerous sighs of relief. Coach would lose his shit if there was fighting.

"Well, that went well," Sammy says loudly, a little too jovial considering the tension. "You think I should run after him and tell him he forgot his training gear?" There's legit glee in his tone.

"That'll be a no." Kieran shakes his head and picks up Jones's gear.

"Why are you picking up his shit?" Ty's still close to Kieran, his guard not yet down. "You should leave it so Coach gives him hell."

Kieran shoves the gear in the cubby assigned to Jones. "What's the point in more antagonism? Before we know it, it's going to be game time. The last thing I want is any lingering bullshit."

And this is why Kieran is such an amazing captain. But I'm with Ty on this. The sooner Jones is off the team, the better for all of us.

Looking at me, Kieran asks, "You okay?"

I huff out a breath. "Yeah. Just could do without an asshole on the team." *And he needs to lay the fuck off Tiller.*

"I hear you, but it's Coach's call."

"Yeah, but he sure wants Leon's spot," Sammy adds. "Jealous as fuck about the support our boy's getting." He claps me on the back. "I've got you, Lee Lee."

His ridiculousness tugs a snort out of me, and I shove him away with a laugh. "Lucky me," I tease, grinning when he winks at me.

"Best get your asses into gear if you want to get breakfast before classes."

At Kieran's words, we focus on finishing up,

leaving together to grab some calories before I have to activate my brain.

I shrug aside Jones's resentment. My place is secure, and Sammy's right, my brothers have my back. It won't be much longer until Coach reaches his limit with Jones, and then things can go back to being chill.

---

Today's earlier bullshit seems so insignificant.

After I met Tiller, we grabbed a bite to eat before heading back to my place. We've made out, got all hot and bothered, which leads us to now.

And honestly, I don't know what to say.

Being responsible and finally having "the talk" was awkward enough a while back, but we're now discussing going without condoms, something I really want. This then led to Tiller's disclosure and his clear embarrassment, and I'm kind of speechless.

I don't want to offend him.

I certainly don't want him to feel bad, and there's absolutely nothing to be ashamed about.

"This isn't the sexiest conversation ever, huh?" An awkward, self-deprecating laugh follows his words.

"Hey." I clamp my hand on his knee and squeeze.

We're on my bed, fully dressed and semi-facing each other. "I think being honest with each other can be totally sexy." I dip down to catch his gaze. When I have it, I smile. "That must have been shit. Thanks for telling me."

It makes even more sense now why he asked me about our health—and being negative—before that first time we blew each other.

"It was." A humorless laugh follows, but his gaze is soft as he leans into my space.

Without hesitation, I meet him, welcoming his tender kiss.

I feel his whole body sag, his relief palpable.

"We don't have to talk about it if you don't want to," I offer. While I want to know, I can wait until he's ready to share more with me.

"Thanks." He dots another kiss against my lips and eases away. This time, he presses close to my side and holds my hand as we lean against my headboard.

"My ex gave it to me."

My brows lift in surprise.

"He gave you an STI?" Does that mean—

"Yeah, I was surprised too. We'd been together for over eighteen months. At least half of that time he was fucking around."

There's no venom in his voice. Everything is matter-of-fact. But hell, that must have hurt.

"Jesus. He sounds like a piece of work."

"He was. Played me for a fool too."

His voice is giving nothing away. I need to look at him.

I angle toward him so I'm sitting sideways, still holding his hand, my knees touching his thigh as I sit cross-legged.

"I didn't come out to my parents until the night before the draft pick."

Holy shit. The draft pick he abandoned.

"Curtis, my ex, agreed to keep our relationship secret, though he wasn't closeted. He was a fucking hoop ho, though."

"Oh shit."

"Yeah. Not that I realized at the time. He manipulated me, gaslighted me into believing I was nothing without basketball. He pretty much coerced me into entering the draft. Fuck." He shakes his head, the first sign of anger threading through his words.

Hurt for Tiller makes my breath catch. Curtis deserves all the karma in the world poured down his throat.

"I hope his dick burns off." The words rush out of me, full of venom and completely not what I intended to say, but when a loud laugh bursts out of Tiller, I don't regret how ridiculous my response was. I shrug at him, grateful to see lightness in his gaze. "Poetic, I know."

He snorts. "That would be pretty epic karma."

"To start with."

I'm totally serious, and from the smile Tiller gifts me, I figure he knows that.

"Anyway, it was a shitfest. Between being manipulated into joining the draft and being a League player, to then discovering him being unfaithful, then with the STI, it all came to a head. I told my parents everything."

Hell, just the thought of that conversation makes me wince.

"I thought it was going to be bad as well," Tiller says, gaze roaming my expression. "I know Dad can be a hardass."

"Uh-huh." No way am I coming out and agreeing with that statement, no matter how correct Tiller is.

He's still smiling as he says, "But my parents are pretty amazing. If anything, they were devastated that they didn't realize something was wrong."

"That must have been hard. On all of you," I clarify.

"It was. Just the thought of going pro made me ill. I've never wanted it. I know that makes me sound crazy—"

"No." I shake my head. "Not at all. I get it." And I do. While I'm not a shoo-in like Kieran, if I'd wanted the League, I think I could have made it. Maybe I would have been pick number fifty-seven or something, but still. "There's a special kind of wiring, of mindset needed to go pro. It's not me. I love the game, but it's not my life."

"I love it, too, and I kind of want it to be my life."

"Coaching." The answer is right there for me. "You're an incredible coach."

Pink spreads across his cheeks. "Yeah?"

"Fuck yes. You're incredible. So damn patient. And you care, you know. You want to make a difference."

The pink staining his cheeks turns to a deep red. "I do."

"Then I have no doubt you'll make it happen."

We've talked about my plans for the future, which, honestly, aren't stuck in stone. I've got nothing set up yet, and I don't intend to pull my finger out until after the basketball season is over.

Is it bad that I hope Tiller will keep kicking his heels playing barista rather than searching for a full-time position that could take him who knows where? By then, at the end of college, just maybe we can line things up to be close by. Hell, in the same apartment even.

"What are you thinking?"

It's my turn to feel the spread of heat.

While there's no way I'm going to tell him exactly where my head's at, I land on "Just thinking about the future and where we might end up."

He can take from that what he will.

From his sweet smile and the whisper of heated promise in his gaze, I kinda hope his brain is fast-forwarding to what comes next too.

# CHAPTER 12
## TILLER

It's hard not to stare at Leon. It's difficult enough during practice when he owns the court, but when he's chewing the end of a pen, gaze intent on the book he's taking notes from, he's ludicrously sexy.

For the past two weeks, we've been together every downtime we've had. His housemates don't even do a double take anymore, which makes it even easier to be in Leon's space. It helps that I like all his friends, and I get the impression they don't mind me hanging around.

"Stop it." Leon's words are barely above a whisper since Sammy and Bentley are spread out on the couch opposite us. They're talking, though, so I don't think they're paying any attention.

"Stop what?"

His gaze meets mine, one of his brows arching. "You know exactly what."

I grin because I absolutely do. I've been mentally undressing him for the past half hour while willing him to hurry up so we can make an excuse to disappear. I haven't seen him for three days. Sure, we've texted and talked, but I'm desperate to get my mouth on him.

I'm also eager to see if he's ready for more. After yesterday's video call, when we both jacked off while I described in great detail how much I want him to fuck me, I desperately hope he's up for it. With my extra prep before coming out tonight, plus the condoms I packed just in case he wants to change his mind and the tube of lube in my pocket, I'm raring to go.

"You got much more to do?" I ask, indicating the textbook.

He studies me for a beat, gaze roaming mine before trailing down my body. I'm of half a mind to pull out the tube in my pocket as an incentive, but I have to at least pretend to have some self-control.

"Fifteen minutes," he says with a smirk.

I huff a breath and inch closer to his side, wanting to feel his heat. Yeah, I know this means we're touching, and a couple more inches, I'd be sitting on him, but since Sammy's lounging on the couch with his head on Bentley's lap, I'm not too worried. The first time I'd seen just how touchy-feely these guys were, it was hard to look away. I even asked Leon if something was going on with them, but his furrowed brow and bewildered "Fuck no" nipped that theory in the bud. That's not to say I'm convinced.

With Leon's thigh pressed against mine, I relax, enjoying the warmth. I've been ridiculously needy since the moment we met, but I'm embracing the rightness of being with him. We've talked about everything. I even told him about what happened at college and the League. Admittedly, discovering he has no plans to go pro made the conversation so much easier, effectively opened the gates, my past practically rushing out.

I feel better for it, more relaxed. And that he passed no judgment, beyond what a fucker my ex is, chipped away some of the hurt that had refused to budge.

"Has it been fifteen minutes yet?" I aim for innocence, but Leon's quirked brow tells me he's not buying it.

Refocusing on his textbook, he pointedly ignores me. He even pays no attention to my roaming hand that dips behind his back, where I trail my fingers beneath his T-shirt and stroke his spine.

Movement from the couch draws my attention.

Both Sammy and Bentley stand, their gazes traveling to us.

"I'm beat and going to have an early night," Sammy says. He does look a little tired; not surprising, since training was full-on today. His yawn, though, is completely fake. I hold back my chuckle, convinced that something is going on between them.

Interested to see what Bentley has to say, I bob my head at Sammy, then look at Bentley.

"Uhm… I have shit to do." With a dip of his head, he walks out of the room, leaving a bemused Sammy behind.

Still holding back the need to laugh, I bite the insides of my cheeks before controlling myself and saying goodnight to Sammy.

"Do you seriously not see that?" I squeeze Leon's waist when we're alone.

"Huh? See what?"

I frown and shake my head, bewildered that he's oblivious. "Nothing," I say. There's little point in pushing this; it's not my business. I follow up with "We're alone" as I settle my hand on his knee.

I take great delight in walking my fingers up his thigh, inching closer to his bulge. When his breath hitches, I go in for the kill and press my lips against his neck. Leon angles so I can get better access. Smiling against his skin, I inhale his freshly showered scent before licking a trail up his neck. "How's that fifteen minutes looking?"

"Done," he answers breathlessly. "I'm all done."

Pulling back, I chuckle, standing up quickly before he can change his mind. I reach for his hand, my gut tightening when he peers up at me. Desire fills his features, and Jesus, I love it when he looks at me this way.

"Ready while the coast is clear?"

He nods and gets to his feet before leading me out of the sitting area and to his room.

Once the door's locked, I back him to his bed while stripping him down.

"Feeling needy?" He quirks his brow.

"You could say that."

"I like you needy."

"You can make me even needier before making our night, if you want." I tug my hoodie off and get undressed now that Leon is naked.

His cock bobs as curiosity and heat fill his gaze. "Yeah? And how do you propose I do that?"

Despite my hammering heart, I don't pause or hesitate. Swiping my hoodie off the floor, I search the pocket and tug out my supplies.

Wide-eyed, Leon stares at the tube and the condom. His mouth parts, and he swipes his tongue over his bottom lip. It's how his breathing picks up speed and the step he takes to get in my space that lets me know he's ready for this. "You want me inside you?"

Fuck, did you hear how breathy he sounds? My dick jerks, liking it a lot.

"Yeah, I do."

He smiles before wrapping himself around me.

I barely have time to throw the lube and condom on the bed before I'm mauling him. Or maybe he's mauling me? All I know is we're a tangled mess of limbs as I kiss him so thoroughly that my head spins.

"I want you so much," he says with a gasp, his gruff tone sweeping over me and creating goose bumps.

"So have me," I whisper, tugging him to the bed and easing him on top of me.

For a beat, hesitation appears in his gaze. "I...." Leon swallows hard, his nerves making my heart sing and gut clench. Fuck, he's so sexy. "I want to do this right."

I nod and haul him closer, pressing my lips to his. Stopping the kiss, I stroke his cheek. "Everything you do will be perfect. I want you inside me."

He searches my gaze and finally smiles. "Okay." Kneeling between my legs, he shakily picks up the lube, squirting some on his fingers. "If there's something I do wrong...."

"I'll guide you, but you've got this." Conviction bleeds through my words, and fuck, he doesn't disappoint when he slips a finger inside me, his eyes wide as he worries his lip.

"Fuck, that's so hot." Awe fills his voice, and he flicks his gaze to my face.

A soft sigh escapes, and I smile. "Add another."

Leon grunts and does as I say, working me open with gentle, probing fingers. I groan into his touch. It's been so long since I've trusted someone like this. I've missed the feeling, missed the pressure.

"Another," I gasp, urging him on, my hips jolting, searching for more.

"Like this?" Gone is the uncertainty of a few moments ago. I expect me practically writhing on the bed clues him in to how good this feels and how much I want him. His thick fingers stretch me wide, and I know he's searching, looking for the spot that's an enigma to him. I can't wait until I get the chance to return this experience so I can watch him light up.

"Yeah." A gasp races out of me when he brushes against my prostate. "Fuck." My vision wavers, cock filling again after flagging from the intrusion of his fingers.

"What's it feel like?" He leans over and licks at my chest, fingers still working me over.

"Like you've lit a fire inside me," I say with a

fresh moan. "Like I can't imagine doing this with anyone but you."

Leon shudders before kissing me deeply. His kiss is slow and exploring; it also stops his delving fingers, giving me the chance to breathe and ease back from blowing my load.

Pulling away with a gasp, he says, "I want this with you so badly. Are you ready for me?"

"Yeah." I'm back to stroking his cheek. When he angles away and reaches for the condom, I settle my palms on his thighs, squeezing lightly. I need to center myself and engrave every moment into my brain.

"Do you want me to use this?"

I shake my head. "No." We've had the conversation. I'm on PrEP, and more than anything, I trust him.

With a smile, he tosses the condom to the side. Once he's lubed, he presses against my opening. With his brows furrowed, Leon's breathing turns ragged. He doesn't know where to look, glancing from my face to my ass almost frantically.

"Hey," I say gently.

When our gazes meet, he takes a deep breath, and I smile. His lips curve before he pushes into me. And fuck, it's hard not to close my eyes and disappear into the sensation. But I don't want to miss a thing.

Leon enters me so slowly that I think I might go insane, his dick stretching me to the point that I'm gasping and going cross-eyed. I love every slide of his cock, every groan he makes, and how perfectly I burn around him.

"Fuck," he grunts when he bottoms out. "You okay?" Leon's voice is tight. It sounds like he's struggling to hold on.

"Yeah. I just need you to move." I clamp on to his hips. "Fuck me."

As if those words are the trigger he needs, Leon smiles widely before easing back and slamming into me. He doesn't hold back. Thank fuck. He pounds into me, gaze unwavering for long seconds as he pushes harder with steady thrusts on shaky arms.

My gasps are probably too loud, but I can't find it in me to care. Not with Leon's sure strokes, not with the graze of his cock over my prostate.

"So fucking good." The praise spills out of him with a soft moan. "I want you to do this to me," he says, his eyes wild, "so fucking much."

I shudder under him, lifting my hips, taking him deeper. "I want that too." I grip my cock and jack myself, wanting so much to come with Leon inside me.

He watches my hand and buries his teeth in his

bottom lip. "You close?" he asks after a few more thrusts.

I nod, struggling to answer.

"Thank fuck."

I want to snort, but my head's spinning, and heat's building in the base of my spine, making it impossible to form words.

Pushing harder and so deep I'm not sure where I end and he begins, Leon shudders before his body becomes taut. My groan is loud as heat races through me, my release pushing to the surface.

Stars explode, swarming my vision as my toes curl almost to the point of pain. But pain like this, fuck, I'll happily take it every single day, every chance I'm lucky enough to share this with Leon.

I'm still not seeing straight when his solid body presses down on me, forcing me to tug my hand away from my spent dick. Somehow I find the energy to wrap my arms around his sweaty back. His breathing is loud against my neck, causing fresh goose bumps.

"You okay?" I manage to ask, holding him tighter when he kisses the sensitive spot below my ear.

"Other than not feeling my legs, I'm fucking amazing." Another kiss follows. "*You're* amazing." He nuzzles against me, seemingly getting comfortable.

I chuckle, earning a groan as I tighten around him.

"Fuck, let me pull out."

I reluctantly agree, despite liking how he feels buried inside me. "If you must."

Pulling away with a smirk, Leon looks thoroughly pleased. "I'll happily visit this ass of yours whenever you want." He kisses me before reaching for some tissues on his bedside table. He rakes his gaze over me, settling on the mess on my stomach. "If we're sneaky, we should be able to get a shower in."

"Together?"

Some of the glaze lifts from his eyes, becoming heated. "Hell yes. I can't handle you being naked in my house without being with you."

Warmth unfurls in my stomach at his admission. "I like this plan."

"Me too," he says before tugging me out of bed.

# CHAPTER 13
## LEON

Being with Tiller is as easy as a basic dribble and drive. And just like I always follow through on the court, I absolutely do with Tiller too.

Our feet are tangled on top of the bedsheets. While I'm doing some reading for an assignment, Tiller's watching through last year's game footage. He's super focused on the video of our championship game against the Bluehawks. The small crease between his eyebrows is cute, and the way his eyes dart across the laptop screen is endearing.

Yeah, I'm totally gone for the guy. The fact that I think everything he does is adorable is a huge tell.

"I can feel you watching me."

Since I've been busted, I turn more toward him and peer up. "You're much more interesting than these tedious articles on business management."

Pausing the footage, he grins down at me. "Doesn't seem like much of a contest, but I'll take it."

I settle my hand on his stomach, absorbing the heat of his skin through his thin T-shirt. Not touching Tiller is almost impossible when he's in my orbit.

A thud has me looking at the door, even though the noise is definitely coming from Ty's bedroom. My lips twitch. "And how about *that* development?"

Tiller's eyebrows jerk high as he says, "Right! And you seriously didn't know?"

I shrug a little lazily, and maybe a little guiltily too. "In fairness, Ty hasn't really spoken much about his sexuality, and when he did the one time, I kind of zoned out." At the wrinkling of his brow, I rush to add, "I know, I know. I'm a sucky friend. But in my lousy defense, he went into fact-giving mode and confused the fuck out of me. And Ty's just... Ty." I shrug. "He's just so together and shares exactly what he wants."

Tiller's soft hum has me frowning.

"What?"

"Just... I know Ty has the whole genius thing going on, and he seems really fucking happy, but that level of intensity can come with a boatload of pressure." A flicker of sadness appears in his gaze. I don't like it one bit, especially as I imagine he's thinking about his own college experience and his ex.

"You're right." I lift and press a kiss to his mouth, wanting to erase his frown. "I admit I've been caught up pretty spectacularly in this man who's snagged my attention." While I'm flirting, I know I haven't been a great friend of late. All my spare time has been spent with Tiller. "I have no regrets about that," I clarify. But it would be so much easier if we shared our relationship with my housemates, at least.

I want to say as much, but I don't want to put pressure on Tiller or what's happening between us. Plus, I'd be asking my friends to keep our relationship a secret. I don't want them caught up in any potential drama with Coach.

Not that I think there's going to be drama necessarily, but still, the fact that I'm dating the Coach's son feels… I don't know. Not wrong. Never that. But a bit sketchy, maybe. And awkward. Definitely awkward.

Tiller shifts, pushing his laptop toward the foot of the bed. Once his hands are free, he returns to me, his head on my pillow so we're face-to-face. "I don't like keeping our relationship on the down-low."

There's a spike in my pulse. There always is when he reads me so well.

"I can talk to my dad—"

"Not yet," I interrupt, and fuck, his brows furrow. Hurt flashes in his gaze. Reacting immediately, I wrap an arm around him, inching forward until our thighs are flush but I can still see his face. "What I'm going to say is completely irrational, I think, and will probably sound all levels of ridiculous." Heat crawls up my neck, and with Tiller's confusion battling his hurt, I've never felt more fucking immature.

Jesus. Whoever said twenty-two means I'm a grown-ass man didn't know what they were talking about.

"What is it?"

At least his tone is soft. Between Tiller's gentle voice and him moving his hand to my waist, I remember I have an impressive pair of balls and, despite my embarrassment, find the will to say, "I... I suppose I just don't want to rock the boat."

He blinks once, twice, and I know he's waiting for more.

The heat in my cheeks jumps another thirty degrees. "What we have..." I want to roll my eyes at how fucking flustered I am. This is real, as in soul-bearing grown-up talk, but fuck if I don't feel like I'm out of my depth. "It's new." Once again his brow furrows, since we, as in the two of us together, aren't *that* fucking new. Knowing I'm being as clear as mud, I'm quick to clarify, "As in this feeling... me dating anyone."

Tiller knows I've had one semiserious girlfriend, and that was back at high school.

"And…" I exhale and want to shake myself silly. "I really like you. Like, a fucking lot. And I don't want to screw it up. Once everyone knows, I'm sure there's going to be comments. And not about me being bi. Well, there might be, but anyone who has anything to say about my sexuality can go fuck themselves."

I'm rambling. All my thoughts that I hadn't fully processed or even really contemplated spill out of me like a tsunami of oversharing emotions.

"I just want to stay in this bubble."

There's more I could say about my friends, but between my frantic pulse and Tiller's sweet and tender smile, my TMI runs its course.

The gentlest of caresses has me sighing as his thumb strokes my cheek. His fingers are cool on my flaming skin.

"Whenever you're ready to tell everyone is more than okay. I'm ready now or a month from now."

"Yeah?"

"Yeah."

I nod and swallow at the flicker of desire in his gaze. It's a look I've become so familiar with. Honestly, since the moment we met and made eye contact the weekend before school started, I've seen it. Only now, on top of desire, there's a deep connection.

"And for the record, I really fucking like you too."

A fizz of happiness bubbles in my stomach, shooting small sparks of pleasure right on up until they ping around my thundering heart.

Caring for Tiller is easy.

The only thing that's going to be hard is continuing to act like he's not close to becoming the most important part of my world.

Once I get my head wrapped around the intensity of my feelings, I figure I'll be ready to shout from the bleachers just how important Tiller is to me.

# CHAPTER 14
## TILLER

For three weeks, I've been ducking questions from my parents. They're on my case, wondering where I'm spending all my time. It's all a little alien to me.

I haven't lived at home for seven years, so I think we're all trying to learn to live together again, but at some point, I figure Leon and I will have to come clean.

My worry is I still don't know how Dad will react to me dating one of his players.

Leon and I seem to have skipped through the awkward ritual of figuring out whether we're just hanging out or friends with bennies, and I'm thankful for it. Being with him is easy and fun. I like everything I'm learning about him, and spending time with him is the best part of my day.

The sex is spectacular too. He's curious and wants to try everything.

Our relationship is also seriously making me reconsider what to do next.

When I left Indonesia, I had no plans beyond spending time with my parents. I missed them. I also felt more at peace with my decisions years back and no longer had the urge to run and hide.

But whether that means I'm going to put my degree to good use, the jury's still out. The thought makes me twitchy, while easing some of the tension I've been carrying.

"What are you huffing about over there?" Mom asks, walking into the sitting room where I'm flicking through Netflix.

Since I didn't realize I'd been making noises, I shrug before turning off the TV. I'm waiting for Dad to get his ass into gear, as he's driving me to practice. I'm also frustrated because Leon's got study plans after training, so we don't get to hang out.

Maybe I should pick up a second job or something. Keeping busy will help distract me from all the times I can't see Leon. I'm so needy it's on the verge of pathetic, but did I mention how much I like the guy?

"You know, if you're bored, you could get a

hobby or maybe go out and see some of your old friends."

"Maybe. I'm not really in touch with anyone local," I deflect. Sure, there's my cousin Michael, but he's recently started dating. There's also a reason I haven't stayed in touch with people from high school.

"How about reaching out to some of your college friends?" She takes a seat next to me. "You haven't seen anyone since being back home. It'll probably do you good."

I raise my brows as I take her in. She's already in her pj's and has a paperback tucked under her arm. It's the easiest way for her to unwind after a busy work shift. She's a pathology assistant at the local hospital, so she regularly comes home drained.

"Are you saying I look pathetic and need to get out more?"

She shakes her head. "Hardly. I barely ever see you," she says pointedly. "I can't help wondering if someone's holding your interest."

Unbidden, heat burns my cheeks. Mom reacts immediately, grinning widely. "I knew it."

"Nope. You don't know anything." I look at the door, willing Dad to hurry up.

"Okay," she says slowly, "I don't know anything,

but if I did know something or you want to talk about *something*, you can."

My shoulders sag, more than aware that Mom only wants what's best for me. Her excitement is clear, though. When she squeezes my forearm, I meet her gaze. A soft smile is directed at me, though I see concern in her eyes.

"I know you haven't dated for a long time." I somehow hold back my wince as she carries on. "But it's okay to take a chance and trust someone. You can also trust me if you need a sounding board."

Guilt bubbles to life in my chest. Maybe if I'd told Mom I was gay earlier, told her about my ex and let her meet him, she'd have seen through his bullshit. Something I couldn't do.

Discovering Curtis was only with me because I was heading to the League was gutting. Not helped by the fact that I'd shared my soul with him, telling him I didn't want to go to the draft. Didn't want to go pro.

He'd put pressure on me immediately. Made me feel ridiculous for not taking the chance. The fucking hoop ho had played so successfully on my emotions that I hadn't felt able to walk away from going pro… or from him. The whole thing had been a clusterfuck of emotional abuse. Something that took me time to deal with.

It wasn't until I decided to pull out from my number one spot that I broke and told my parents the truth about me. My sexuality. Curtis. How he'd convinced me I was nothing without basketball… or him.

This was after learning he'd messed around on me and given me gonorrhea as a parting gift.

Yeah, that made me say "what the fuck" too. I told you he was an asshole and really leaning into the ho part of hoop ho.

"Thanks, Mom." I lean into her, welcoming her warmth as she hugs me close. Fuck, I've missed her.

She dots a kiss on my head just as Dad enters the room. He pauses in the doorway, gaze assessing. Worry flares to life in his eyes, and I hate that this is their go-to reaction. The last thing I want them to do is worry about me or think I'm ready to bolt.

"All okay in here?"

"Of course," Mom answers. "I'm just getting my hugs in when I can."

I squeeze her a little tighter, appreciating her support so much. Pulling away, I give Dad an up-nod. "You ready to go?"

He studies me before saying, "Sure thing." A smile tilts his lips. "Good to see your uniform fits."

I roll my eyes as I stand, peering down at my Bears staff uniform. It appeared on my bed a couple of days ago, throwing me for a loop with a swell of emotion that clogged my throat. I know it's Dad's way of telling me he's happy I'm back and wants me to stick around. "It does, thanks. Anyone would think you're trying to tell me something," I sass.

Dad grunts before leaning to kiss Mom.

"Are you coming home for dinner?" Mom calls from her position on the couch. Training today starts at three, so we should be back by six at the latest.

I nod. "That's the plan."

Mom smiles. "If you don't, it'll keep, so don't worry about missing it." She bounces her brows. Her subtlety has no game.

After I grab my bag, we head out to the car. Once we're settled, Dad clears his throat and flicks his gaze at me.

I look at him, brows dipping a little at his discomfort.

"I appreciate your help with the training," he says, glancing at me. "You're doing a great job with the team and especially Leon. You've brought something fresh to the game, new pointers and showing them some alternate plays."

Swallowing hard at the pride I hear in his voice, I nod. "Thanks." There's gruffness to my tone. "I've enjoyed helping out, and seeing the subtle shifts in plays is pretty great," I admit. It's been amazing, reaffirming my dream to get into coaching. Having this experience should look good on my résumé, too, should I decide to pull my head out of my ass and go after what I really want.

A sound of acknowledgment comes from Dad. He seems happy with my answer.

"Harry's dad's sick."

"Shit. Like, how sick?" I don't know much about Harry, one of the assistant coaches, beyond him being friendly and willing to share his expertise when I've asked him for advice.

"Sick enough that he needs to fly out to New Zealand. His flight's next week. He's taking twelve weeks of family medical leave."

"Poor guy." My brows dip in sadness.

"It means I need someone to cover for him over the next three months."

The sound of my pulse rushes to my ears, picking up speed when I realize where Dad may be going with this.

"It's just part-time, and your health and sports science degree means you have the education to back you up. Plus, you have experience and player knowledge."

"Holy shit," I whisper, my heart hammering.

"I've already spoken to Barry in admin. He said

he'll make it happen on the grounds that it's a temporary position and such short notice that it'll be more difficult to vet and interview potential replacements."

Shock prevents my ability to respond. Any position like this is so hard to come by, and I'm being given one hell of a free pass here by jumping so many rungs on the ladder. The profession is notoriously hard to get into. The competition for a spot, especially on a championship team, is high.

"So, what do you think?"

"Honestly, I'm a little blown away." I shake my head, fisting my hands to hide the trembling. "I can't believe you've set this up for me. Thank you."

"I wouldn't have thrown your name in the ring if I didn't think you were up for the task. Burt and Cary were supportive of the idea too. They see something in you."

Wide-eyed, I stare at Dad. That he's got the approval of the other assistant coaches makes my head spin.

"Listen, why don't you take tonight, and we'll talk about it tomorrow, but I'll need your decision then, okay?"

Overwhelmed, I nod a little woodenly. "Thanks, Dad. I seriously appreciate everything you've ever done for me."

Pink creeps up Dad's neck, his tell that he's feeling my words. "You're a good kid."

I smile. "I'm twenty-five."

"Like I said, a good kid," he says with a laugh. "I know growing up, you always said you were interested in coaching, but that got sort of sidetracked with… everything."

"Everything" being planning to join the League before bolting.

"This is an opportunity if you want to take it. No pressure," he's quick to add.

Those words uncoil the tightness in my chest.

"You won't be disappointed if I say no?"

"Well," he says, side-eyeing me, "I'll be disappointed for the team, but not in you."

Jesus, who knew my old man could wrangle such feelings in me? Emotion sits heavily on my chest—all happiness and gratitude.

"Tomorrow," I confirm, the only thing I can manage to say without sniffling.

Dad bobs his head and stares hard in front of him, the pink flushing his neck still evident.

I smile as we continue the journey, thinking about this fantastic opportunity. I should take it, right? It feels like one of those once-in-a-lifetime opportunities. It will also mean I get to spend more time with—

Fuck, Leon. I'm dating a Bears player.

That won't be okay, right? I'm sure they've got rules about that sort of stuff. It's not like I can just ask Dad, though. Well, not without talking to Leon first. He's still yet to tell his friends, other than Tyron.

Jesus, why can't everything be beautifully breezy and uncomplicated?

# CHAPTER 15

## LEON

We're edging closer to the start of the game season. I am so fucking here for it.

I'm on my game, my training going so well that I can't wait until we can push our limits. It would be a hell of a thing to take home the championship again.

What a way to end our senior year.

Then there's Tiller. There's no denying my boyfriend has some serious skills. Don't get me wrong—in the bedroom, he's incredible. Hands down, I'm having the best sex of my life. Add in our chemistry and how completely gone for him I am, and beyond the secrecy, life's so perfect.

But it's his skills on the court as an assistant coach —even though that's not technically his title since he's volunteering his time—that are impressive.

Without a doubt, his support has fine-tuned my reactions, my ability to read plays and consider moves.

And while I monopolize his time a little, his pointers and guidance have been felt by the whole team.

The only difficulty I have is keeping my hands to myself and my gaze from eating up every inch of him. This secrecy shrouding our relationship has never been a turn-on. It's never felt "good" or added an excitement factor, but I understand the need for it. At least until Tiller stops volunteering his time.

It'll be less odd, then, when it comes time for me to do the official "meet the parents" dinner, right?

I sure hope so.

The difficulty is I don't want Tiller to stop supporting the Bears, but he doesn't want to work as a barista for the rest of his life. And that opens a whole pool of anxiety that I don't want to get buried under right now.

Not when as soon as I finish tying my laces, I'll get to see him on the court.

Even when we're not together in "boyfriend" mode, I'm still eager for any chance I can spend with him, especially as I have to study after practice. My degree isn't going to ace itself, unfortunately.

"You good?"

Laces tied, I drop my foot and smile at Sammy. "Yeah. You?"

He bobs his head as we walk to the court side by side. "You hear Jones spouting shit?"

My brow furrows. While I'm not surprised by Jones, even though he's been pretty quiet over the past few weeks, I'm surprised I didn't hear him. "When? In the locker room?"

Sammy shakes his head as our basketball sneakers hit the side of the court. "Nah, just before. He was talking to Banks."

Now *that* I am surprised by. Banks, one of the freshman players, has eased into the team well. He trains hard and has even been around our place a couple of times, joining us for pizza night.

"Banks was talking shit too?"

"Hell no."

That's a relief to hear.

"The kid tried to shut him down, but Jones wouldn't give up. It's clear he didn't realize I was outside, waiting for Bentley."

"What was he saying?" I glance around, searching for Tiller. He's there, back to me, talking to Coach. There's an uptick of my pulse. Sure, we've texted throughout the day, but it's not the same as me getting my fill.

"More complaints about never getting the chance of being in the starting five."

I roll my eyes, and Sammy scoffs.

"He'll get his chance." In my freshman year, my ass was on the bench more often than not. I lucked out in the middle of my sophomore year, since Buchanan—our shooting guard—folded with an injury, giving me my shot.

Since then, I've always been a starter.

"Right. The guy's a chronic complainer. This is our last year, where we'll kick ass. It'll then give other guys a shot." Sammy shakes his head. "He was whining like a bitch about you. Banks told him to get over himself and ended up walking away."

"Good for Banks. And as for me, I'll keep giving him something to aspire to."

A loud snort ripples out of Sammy as Coach calls us over. "Yeah, you do that. That'll make him chill out."

I hold back my laughter as we gather around Coach Maple and instead turn my attention to Tiller. As always, he looks delicious. He's also wearing one of the Bears staff shirts. It's hard not to grin, since he looks so adorable. Sure, he's worn a coaching jersey before, but this one has his name embroidered on the chest.

And for the first time, he's wearing matching sweatpants.

The uniform looks good on him.

It'll look even better on my floor.

I search his face, silently encouraging him to glance my way, but his focus is completely on his dad.

Disappointment settles in my chest, but I have no time to lament on it as Coach is dishing out his instructions. Holding my breath, I wait like an overeager fan at a buzzer-beating shot. *Don't let me down, Coach.* Talk about needy, but I need Tiller's gaze and one of his sweet "just for me" smiles.

"Bradford, go with Coach Lacey."

Fuck.

Looks like I'm not getting my wish after all.

With a few of the other guys at my side, I dutifully head toward Assistant Coach Lacey, and we start work on some passing drills.

I'm working on two-man passing with Bentley and am barely paying attention. We've been at this for fifteen minutes, and Tiller is just a few feet away. He's working with Jones, which pisses me off. He doesn't deserve Tiller's expertise, not after all the bitching he keeps doing.

"*Oomph.*" The ball smacks me in the chest. I

scramble for the ball, knowing if the rubber hits the floor, Lacey's going to be on my case.

"Where's your head at?" Concern fills Bentley's features.

"Here," I answer quickly, actively focusing on my friend rather than Tiller and the chuckle coming from him.

Fuck. He's laughing at something Jones is saying, which shouldn't annoy me, I know. Does he not know what a shithead the guy is? I've deliberately not discussed what a turd Jones is with my boyfriend. Yeah, I'm regretting it now.

"Uh-huh." Bentley's quirked brow lets me know he's not buying it. One of the things I respect about my friend, though, is he's an amazing confidant. He doesn't gossip or talk shit. He's a legit gentle giant, always looking out for all of us in that quiet way of his.

If he knew about Tiller, how I feel about him, this would be so much easier.

Maybe it's finally time to loop my housemates—my best friends—in, at least.

That I haven't already is frustrating.

"You want to pass the ball back?"

I bob my head and inwardly cringe when Tiller's deep laughter rolls over me.

It's not like I'm jealous. Okay, it kind of is, but

only because not once has my boyfriend made eye contact. Talk about needy. Me, that is.

I'm ridiculous.

I pass Bentley the ball and try to recenter. Coach Lacey appearing at my side makes that happen pretty damn quickly.

"The two of you with me."

We follow immediately, and I barely hold back my sigh when I see he's leading us to an area set up for core training.

Core training is the worst.

Planks, Russian twists, and work with the medicine ball is hell.

Bentley, though, claps his hands.

He lives for this shit.

"Three-minute rotations," Coach Lacey instructs. "You pause, you start from the beginning."

"Sure thing, Coach." Bentley's smile is wide and real. Asshole. "Together?" he asks me.

"Yeah. Sounds good." Truth is, Bentley is a powerhouse. Keeping up with him will help me get through each exercise. Not necessarily unscathed but hopefully without failing and having to start from scratch.

By the time I'm two minutes into my Russian twists, the last core exercise, my obliques are screaming. Sweat rolls off me, soaking my jersey. My muscles shake, legs barely stable.

"Come on." Bentley knows I'm flagging. "Forty-five seconds."

Jesus. Each second feels like a million.

"Feet up."

I readjust my legs, making sure my feet are no longer dipping toward the ground.

"That's it, Bradford. Almost there."

Not having the energy to complain, I clench my jaw, fighting through the pain as I continue to twist my torso side to side. The medicine ball in my grip is slippery. I clench it tighter, determined not to lose my hold.

"Time," Coach Lacey calls.

I collapse on the ground, flat on my back, breathing hard.

At my side, Bentley chuckles, barely puffed as he takes the medicine ball off me.

"Three minutes to recover, then head to Tiller."

At Lacey's instruction, my already racing heart kicks up a gear. The past twenty minutes I haven't been able to think about anything other than my screaming muscles, so that's something, at least.

Whatever I was feeling, any lingering sulking has well and truly dripped away, right along with my sweat.

"I can't move." I angle to peer at Bentley, who, like the warrior he is, went and collected two bottles of water. He passes me one. "Fuck, you're the best."

"You know it." He smirks as he opens his bottle. "You doing okay down there?"

I ease myself up to sit and take big gulps of water.

Cool and soothing, the water offers relief. Not quite instant, but enough to have the thought of standing up not seem as bad. Another gulp and I finally manage a nod. "Yeah. Next year, no more core training." I chuckle. "It's one thing at least to look forward to."

"Truth." Bentley reaches out for me. I clasp his hand and smile as he tugs me up.

We start in the direction of Tiller, and I relax, taking a deeper breath when he's talking to Coach Maple, and Jones is nowhere nearby.

Is it wrong that I hope Tiller goes easy on me? I'm legit exhausted, and my sweat-soaked jersey feels gross. Either way, at least I'll finally get that smile he reserves just for me.

# CHAPTER 16
## TILLER

FROM THE LOOKS LEON KEEPS THROWING ME, HE KNOWS something is off.

Where there's usually sweet, subtle flirting, I'm all business. I need to talk to him as soon as possible, but tugging him away during practice won't work. The worst thing is I'm doing a shit job of keeping my cool and acting casual, to the point that I'm being overfriendly and helpful to the rest of the team while slamming up the shutters when it comes to Leon.

Freaking out is never a good look, especially when Leon's becoming increasingly pissed off with me. His gaze is stern and unwavering as he stands before me with folded arms.

"You need to go again." I try to relax my tone, but I don't think I manage it based on the tightening of his eyes. "Come in from the left, watch your timing, and get up to speed."

"Right." In that one word, he's telling me to go fuck myself. But since there are a couple of the coaches watching, there's no chance he'll challenge me and risk adding more time on the clock.

I watch as he peels off; meanwhile, I wish I was running a different rotation.

This time he's at game speed, his footwork impeccable. Thank Christ. He makes the play and works with a couple of his teammates, ending with an impressive shot.

I smile, relief coursing through me. "Great job." A glance at the clock tells me it's time to wind down, and not a moment too soon.

Rather than respond, he won't even look at me. The worst thing is this is all my fault. My distance and dickish behavior have come completely out of left field.

"On the line," Coach hollers. I'm trying to separate Dad from Coach while here, figuring it's the most professional thing to do. I just wish I had a better handle on my reactions to Leon.

When all the players line up, I'm relieved Coach doesn't give them sprints. Instead, he reminds them of the friendly game we have set up with a nearby college. "Marcus will let you know the next few days' schedule, as there's been some changes," Coach continues, "so keep an eye on your messages."

The team nods and sensibly doesn't grumble. They're dog-tired and sweaty but listen intently to Coach's words.

When he releases the team, the players make a break for it. I seek out Leon, but he's already gone. Disappointed, I swallow my frustration and head over to Coach, who's standing with Burt. When I reach them, they both nod at me and continue their conversation.

"...to work with the strength coach," Burt says. "Bradford's still not up to speed, but we'll get him there."

Coach nods, then looks at me. "What about Bradford?"

Focusing hard to keep as cool as possible, I bob my head, saying, "Good. He was at match speed with a few pushes. Managed to work out a few plays with him."

"Excellent. I have a meeting on Monday morning, so we have to change a few things. Marcus will send you the details as well. I'll need you to meet with the whole staff Monday afternoon."

I glance at Burt and return his smile. Understandably, they think this is a done deal. What fool would turn down this chance of joining the coaching team officially? And to do so for a college kid I'm dating? Just thinking about Leon that way has my gut churning. He is so much more than a convenient hookup. He's also most definitely not a kid.

Fuck, I need to speak to him.

"Sounds good," I respond, an acceptance if I've ever heard one.

From the moment two and a half hours ago when Dad made me the offer, excitement has bubbled into my stomach and hasn't let up. Not even with my worry about Leon. I'll figure it all out somehow. Having the opportunity handed to me on a silver platter is something I can't ignore. Nor do I want to.

Dreams I've worked hard at burying have risen to the surface. They'd been squashed with scoffs by my ex, and almost everyone thought I was crazy the few times I'd mentioned coaching rather than playing in the League.

Who in their right mind would pass up million-dollar-earning skills on the court to work on the sidelines? Hearing it so often made it easier to smile and agree. Until I'd been pushed into a tailspin and run, leaving all the pressure and hurt behind.

Fuck, I really want this.

Leon's confused frown and eyes filled with pain spark in my mind.

"Da—Coach"—I ignore the heat flushing my

cheeks and Burt's smirk—"I forgot I've got plans, so don't worry about a lift."

Dad's no fool. Just like Mom, he suspects I'm dating, but he hasn't questioned me about it. He studies my face before nodding. Tomorrow is a rare day off for us all, so it's not like I have to rush in the morning. "Let your mom know if you're around for dinner tomorrow night."

I smile. "Will do."

"And we need to talk tomorrow." His unwavering gaze locks me down.

"Yes, sir."

He releases me with an up-nod. I get my ass into gear, and fifteen minutes later, I'm finally heading out. I'm not even outside before I pull my cell out and hit Leon's name. It rings out before his voice mail clicks in. I stare at the phone and frown before hitting his name again. This time it rings twice before his message starts.

Fuck. He's canceling my calls.

I wince, knowing my shitty behavior deserves this reaction. I just hope when I arrive on his doorstep, he doesn't slam the door in my face.

It's a risk, but Leon's worth it, and I think our relationship, despite how new it is, is worth it too. Just a few months of knowing each other is no time at all, but I can't deny chemistry. I can't ignore the fizzle of heat that thrums through me when I think about him, let alone spend time with him.

I'm not on board with letting him go and ending things. I just hope we can figure this out and that the college acknowledges an existing relationship prior to employment. I'll stay up all night if I have to, researching and figuring things out.

That's if Leon's willing.

It's still light out, and there's plenty of students around the campus. While it's not as manic as midday, I still have to dodge groups as they seem to be making their way to the food hall. That's something I definitely don't miss. The food plan when I was at college was pretty grim. Back at home with Mom's cooking is something of a treat. I hope she was serious about plating up my food for tomorrow.

I sigh. Or maybe tonight, if Leon doesn't accept my apology for being an asshole.

I know he has studying to do, but this is something we have to sort out. My deadline is tomorrow. By the time I speak to Dad, I need to have worked out what to say and have all the information to cover my ass.

It doesn't take long to reach Leon's shared house. When I stand outside the door, I shake my hands, wishing I'd sent a text before practice, letting him know I had something important to discuss.

Maybe that would have been enough of a heads-up that something was going on. More than that, though, I wish I hadn't freaked out and behaved like a prick of a drill sergeant. If we figure things out, I have no choice but to do better, *be* better when I'm at work.

Before I get the chance to knock, the door opens. Tyron stands in the doorway, his gaze hard, his expression letting me know he's pissed off at me.

"Is there a reason that you're lurking?"

I huff out a breath. This whole new dynamic thing is going to be hard as fuck. Volunteering has meant it's been more than okay to become friendly with the whole team. I've spent so much time around this place that it's become like a second home. How the hell am I going to navigate that when I step up into an official role?

Inwardly, I roll my eyes at myself. *It's why there are strict codes of conduct for staff and student relationships, jackass.*

"Tyron," I greet, forcing myself to calm. "Is Leon home?"

He studies me a beat before nodding.

When he doesn't speak, I ask, "Is it okay if I come in and speak to him?"

For a few long seconds, he stares me down. Surprising me, he steps back without a word, indicating I should come inside. "He's in his room," he says when he's closed the front door.

"Thanks." As soon as my foot touches the staircase, Tyron calls my name. I glance back at him.

"Managing Nepotism and Personal Relationships."

A frown pulls my eyebrows low. "What?"

"It's one of Brixham's governing policies. It won't take long to read. All you have to do is make sure to report your relationship to Coach, and there's no issue."

My mouth falls open. "How did you—"

When he quirks a brow at me, I slam my mouth shut. Of course he fucking knows. This guy will have known before I did. I swear he has ears and eyes everywhere.

"What did you say you're majoring in again?"

He licks over his top teeth, studying me. I don't miss the slight twitch of his lips. "BS and MS in Criminal Justice and Criminology."

A light huff escapes me.

"And what are you planning on doing with that?"

"Join the FBI."

I jolt in surprise. Is he for real? I can't read this guy at all. "You're shittin' me."

"I shit you not."

"Huh." Speechless, it's all I can manage. I then

think about the information he told me, hope fluttering to life in my chest. "Thanks," I say, wishing I'd had time to start getting answers myself. Since the car journey, everything has played on fast-forward, sending my mind reeling and my emotions spinning.

"Don't fuck this up."

I bob my head in acknowledgment and focus on taking one step at a time before I raise my hand to tap on Leon's door.

Here I go.

# CHAPTER 17

## LEON

SOMETHING'S OFF. I WISH I WAS DESCRIBING THE leftover takeout in the refrigerator, but this stink has the name of Tiller.

As soon as I saw him in training, my gut tightened. Funny how the lack of eye contact can have that effect, right? The added avoidance of looking my way, teamed with his indifference when we were forced to interact, was a big red flag if ever I saw one. You saw it, too, right? Yeah, it was pretty hard to miss.

Logically, I figure something's happened for Tiller to behave this way. After pacing my bedroom and huffing over my laptop, which I can't focus on, I finally understand that. When we were training, however, all I wanted was to get in his space and force him to look at me. For all the obvious reasons, I couldn't do that, which wound me up more and more.

I shove my laptop away from where I'm sitting on my bed. Frustration pulses inside my veins, thrumming an annoying beat. His coldness can't have just come out of the blue for no reason at all.

I flick open our text exchanges from earlier today, pointedly ignoring the missed call notifications.

I've reread them so many times, trying to read between the lines, see if there was something he was holding back... a possible tone I didn't interpret correctly, but there's nothing.

A "miss you" doesn't really make me question anything beyond maybe I'm losing my damn mind. Hell, maybe it's all my imagination. I did admittedly feel jealous earlier. Maybe I read into that.

*Bullshit.*

Yeah, there was no Imagineering his distance. I sigh. Only a conversation will fix this.

Are you wondering how my heart is reacting? Surely you can hear its heavy thud that keeps picking up the pace when I think about Tiller. Never have I wanted someone as much as I want him. And fuck if I don't want to keep him.

We're new-ish. I get it. I'm already imagining all the eye rolls at the declaration clawing to free itself from my heart. But you know what? All those eye rolls can spin around and roll away, ideally while going to fuck themselves.

Tiller makes my heart go wild. He fills it with passion and heat and joy. There's so much room left in there for all the things I still want to discover and learn about the man.

Focusing back on my cell, finally ready to stop ignoring his calls, I pause when I hear a creak on the staircase. Muffled voices carry my way, and while I can't make out the words, I recognize the cadence of both. The lighter, less gravelly voice is impossible not to react to.

He came.

Palms becoming clammy, I stand, quickly wiping them down my sweatpants.

I have to believe he's here to explain himself. The thought of the alternative makes my stomach lurch, but I need to steel myself for the possibility of heartbreak.

Fuck. I hate the thought of that, especially as it smacks me in the face, jumping out of nowhere.

At the soft tap on my door, I swallow hard and flex my fingers, trying to loosen up before opening the door. Warm eyes latch on to mine. Concern and wariness radiate from their depths, but I can't move.

"Can I come in?" he asks, his tone quiet, wary. "I

know you have to study, so I won't stay unless you want me to."

The admission unravels some of the tension curled around me. *He'll stay if I want him to.* That's a good sign, right?

"Sure." I step back and hold his gaze as he walks past me. "I couldn't concentrate, so you're not interrupting." I close the door as he hesitates next to my bed. "You can sit down."

A small smile lifts his lips as he bobs his head. "So… I was an asshole."

More tension unravels, and I snort. "You think?"

"I freaked the fuck out."

I make my way over to the bed to sit beside him, my confusion building with every step. "About what?"

"About how to behave, how to not treat you in a way that shows everyone how much I care about you."

He steals my breath with his admission. "Yeah?"

Placing his palm on the bed, he extends his pinkie, searching for mine. "Yeah," he says as I loop my finger around his. "I've been offered a temporary position on the coaching team."

Surprise jolts me. "Holy shit. That's incredible." Wide-eyed, I stare at him, happiness springing to life that he finally has the opportunity to explore coaching to see if this may be something he really wants to do. But he's not smiling. "Are you not happy about the offer?"

"No, I am. Like, it's fucking amazing. I know I've only got an in because of Dad."

"That doesn't mean you won't be brilliant at it. You've proven yourself since being here, and your degree set you up for this, right? Not to mention you still hold records. That's all you, not your dad."

Loosening my finger, he pulls my hand into his, holding it properly. There's a sweet shyness in the way he's looking at me that melts my heart. Fuck, I'm so gone for him.

"Thanks," he whispers. The way he swallows, gaze unwavering, it's clear he has more to say. Squeezing his hand, I wait him out, giving him silent encouragement. "It means I'll be employed by the college. Officially a member of staff."

He lets the words hang there. It only takes a beat before what he's not saying slams into me. The pounding in my ears is immediate. "Fuck. And I'm a student." Watching, waiting, Tiller remains silent. "Does that mean we can't…?" Not wanting to voice the question, I trail off.

A tight lift of Tiller's lips follows, along with a slight wince. "We can"—my heart leaps—"but it'll mean reporting the relationship."

My breath whooshes out of me. The drumming in my ears picks up.

When I don't speak, worry sparks in his eyes. "The last thing I want to do is put pressure on you. Fuck, it kills me to."

The pain in his voice breaks through my panic, and I grip his hand, understanding where his distress is coming from. Thoughts about his reasons for not joining the League and bailing filter through me. The way he felt bulldozed, and even though he didn't use the word, I'm smart enough to know what emotional abuse looks like.

"No." I force certainty into my words. "This is nothing like what you went through. I still have a choice and a decision. And I know you'd never push me into one."

"I wouldn't." He shakes his head. "I didn't say yes straight away either."

My eyebrows shoot high before they furrow in confusion. "You didn't?"

"No. I wanted to talk to you first. I have until tomorrow."

Sweat breaks out in the middle of my back. "You'd turn down the job if I didn't want you to disclose our relationship?" Heaviness pushes against my chest, and I shake my head. "No fucking way.

You can't turn down this opportunity because of me. I—"

"Hey." Tiller shifts and straddles me, calming my rising panic. "I just wanted to talk this through with you first. There was no grand plan. No 'if you don't, then I will' scenario. This is just me wanting to talk about this opportunity with my hot boyfriend."

I can't help it. Despite the seriousness and the push of panic, I smirk. "Hot, huh? And grown-up relationship conversations… shit, man, that's one way to make my dick hard."

Laughter fills the small space between us. The sound relaxes my shoulders, and I wrap my arms around Tiller, holding him close, my face pressed against his chest.

We stay like this for a while, Tiller pressing soft kisses to the top of my head, me listening to his calming heartbeat.

"We're not doing a great job at hiding our relationship from my housemates," I say with a smile.

"Me being here and disappearing with you is kinda giving that away, huh?"

"You're also pretty loud," I sass.

He snorts against my hair before angling back to look at me.

In all seriousness, while Ty has done me proud keeping his knowledge about my relationship with

Tiller to himself, my friends' smirks and Kieran's offer to chat whenever I'm ready have been constant. But they're giving me space to work things through, and I appreciate them all the more for it.

"I'm ready to hold your hand in public." Embarrassment warms my cheeks. "Fuck, I sound like a dickhead, right?"

Tiller's grin is blinding. He palms my cheek and dots a kiss on my lips. "I'm more than ready to hold your hand whenever you want."

"You are?"

"You know how hard it's been not kissing you?"

I shake my head, happy to play coy and hear his sweet words.

"Do you not remember how we met?"

My smile at the memory is instant. Hell, I'd kissed him in public then, not giving a shit. Fuck knows how that didn't blow up the gossip mill. "Since it pretty much changed everything for me, I don't think I'll ever forget."

The way he strokes my cheek makes my pulse ramp up. Tenderness flares in his gaze when he says, "I have a thing for PDA." Tiller quirks an eyebrow high. "So hand-holding, kisses, hugs… you want them, you don't even need to ask." He sweeps his thumb across my bottom lip, and I dart my tongue out, loving the hitch in his breath when the tip touches his skin.

"How about in the middle of training?" I tease.

"Ha. Maybe not when I'm at work, but I'm all yours as soon as the time is up."

"You are, huh?" I say, my happiness swelling at the mention of him working. He'll be amazing in the position.

"For as long as you'll have me."

Holy shit, please tell me you melted like I did. With Tiller on my lap, I'm a puddle of emotion. Instead of answering, I tell him how I feel with a press of my mouth against his. The kiss is sweet and tender and full of my relief that we're okay and confidence that being with him is absolutely the right decision.

Breathless, I pull away. Tiller's pupils are blown. While it would be easy to strip him down and seal this decision in my favorite way, I need to do this next thing. Plus, there's that shitty studying to do. "You want to try that hand-holding now and go downstairs and grab a snack?"

"Do you have a full house?"

I nod, smiling even though my nerves are tripping over themselves.

His gaze searches mine before he smiles. "Absolutely."

I chase one last kiss before he climbs off me. Then, hand in hand, we head downstairs, where all my housemates are hanging out.

Holy shit. This is really happening.

I'll just ignore the fact that Tiller is going to have a conversation with my coach before the night's through.

# CHAPTER 18

## TILLER

We decided it was best for me to talk to my dad alone. The last thing I want is for Leon to feel any more awkward than he already does about his ball-busting coach being my dad.

And I get it. I really do.

There's been zero discussion about when I'll meet Leon's parents yet. And I think that's totally normal, right? Partly that's because he's waiting to have a face-to-face with them to come out—something he assures me will be a nonissue apparently.

I hope he's right, for his own sake.

Building up your expectations for how things are going to play out, only to have the rug swept from right out under you, is a shit of a thing.

But I trust that he knows his parents, and I love that he's so confident. I'm deliberately keeping the bubbling apprehension to myself. I'm here for him. As long as I remind him of that constantly, it's all I can do.

Well that, and I suppose offer to go home with him on his next visit, which is going to be Thanksgiving.

Do I foresee us still being together then?

For real, that whole speech he made a few weeks ago still kicks up my pulse. You know the one where he told me he likes me. A fucking lot. Yeah, I'm weak at the knees for Leon. It makes my fuckup at training even worse.

That he forgave me so easily, listened to me without interruption… I have no idea what I did to deserve him, but I'm grateful he did.

The front door's not even closed when Mom calls out, "Dinner's in the refrigerator!"

"Thanks, Mom." No chance I can stomach anything yet. Not until I've spoken to Dad. "Where's Dad?" I ask, leaning into the sitting room where she's curled up on the couch with a glass of wine.

"In the den."

I bob my head. "Thanks." Before I step out of the doorway, she calls my name, stopping me.

"You okay?"

Does that mean I look as on edge as I feel? Probably.

After Leon and I headed hand in hand into his sitting room, then took a seat, thigh to thigh and his palm on my knee, there'd been just one giant grin from Sammy, hollering, "Called it," before Tyron threw a cushion at him, responding, "You so did not." Bentley sat quietly, offering a small smile, while Kieran and Dean and beamed broadly, only for the conversation about jelly beans to continue on.

Their easy acceptance was refreshing. Sure, I'm superaware of my position, but I know I can maintain professional distance when it matters.

Today's training session being the only exception. And I'll make sure it stays that way.

After that, Tyron talked Leon and me through the Managing Nepotism and Personal Relationships policy. Thank fuck he did.

It means that professionally and legally I know where I stand. But I still don't know how Dad's going to take it.

"Yeah, good, thanks."

Mom studies me, lips pursed, eyes roaming. "Hmm."

I have a good idea what that hum means, but my nerves are already on edge, so I smile and dash away before she can collar me.

Dad's den is pretty much what you'd expect from a "dad's den"—when the dad in question is a basketball coach. Not only is it decked out with his workspace, but there are four La-Z-Boys, a kickass 98" TV, a minibar with a beer fridge I used to sneak Bud from when I was seventeen, and an arcade basketball table. You know, one of those with a couple of small hoops and you can compete against each other?

Since being home, I've only hung out with Dad a couple of times down here. A little guilt blossoms in my chest that I haven't spent more time with him.

Sure, I see him at practice, but I've been happily dedicating all my time to Leon.

Maybe if this conversation isn't a trainwreck, Leon and I can hang out here with him for a night and watch a game if it doesn't clash with the college program.

Not sure how Leon will feel about that, but hell if I don't like the idea.

"Hey, Dad, you got a minute?"

Dad's at his workstation, which are a couple of large desks pushed together, complete with a huge computer monitor, and plenty of space for him to sketch out his plays.

"Of course." He stretches and pulls off his reading glasses. "You want a beer? I was just finishing up."

"That'd be great, thanks."

I step farther into Dad's domain, taking in the

wall of team photographs, as well as several of me playing college ball.

"It seems like a lifetime ago," I say as he joins me and passes me a bottle of beer. I lift my drink in thanks, and we knock them together before I take a long pull.

"To you maybe." He shrugs, his gaze on a framed article about me holding the record for single-game steals.

There's a moment of quiet as we look over the wall. I feel like such a different person since I left college. Having ventured off and explored so much while being so self-reliant makes the twenty-one-year-old me in the article's photograph seem so young.

So lost.

"Do you regret it?"

Not sure what Dad's referring to, I side-eye him. He turns his head and peers at me.

"Playing college ball," he clarifies. There's a tightness in his tone I've only heard once before. That was the day before I walked away from the life intended for me. The sound, the sadness weaving its way through the tightness, pulls at my chest.

Three years have gone by, and we've still yet to really talk about this.

At the time of me coming out, the focus was on

my mental well-being—and getting me to a clinic for a script for STI treatment—rather than everything else.

Despite Dad's reputation of being a stern, take-no-shit coach, he's still my dad. Not once did he push me to suck it up or simply give the League a go. That may have been because I'd been fractured, a broken mess of hurt, but still… his love, his hug, him listening to me, convincing Mom that me venturing off into the world and finding myself with no hesitation meant everything. It still does.

It makes my second-guessing telling him about Leon even more frustrating.

He doesn't deserve my nervousness.

"I don't regret it," I say quietly. "I love the game." A soft chuckle precedes "I've got my old man to thank for that." I nudge him, the move earning me a relieved huff of laughter.

"When you told me everything you went through —" He clears his throat, and I try not to fidget. "— well, needless to say I pissed your mom off by making it about me and blaming myself for putting too much pressure on you." This time his laugh is self-depreciating, on the cusp of humorless.

"You didn't." At his arched eyebrow, I press my lips together, huff out a breath, and land on "Well, not deliberately. You always told me I had options."

He had. Dad didn't shut down the discussion about me coaching. "I just... you were so damn proud." I shrug. "You were my first ever coach. I had the skill to make it."

"But it wasn't for you," he finishes.

"No." I shake my head. "And with my sexuality, my ex."

Ever predictable, my dad scowls. For the first time ever, his reaction pulls a laugh from me. It's loud and real and so fucking good.

"I love you, Dad. Never quite knew you had the protective streak you have until you threatened to find Curtis and cut his 'rotten' dick off."

Dad splutters out his beer, not covering his mouth quick enough to stop it from spraying on the floor.

My laughter rings through the den as I pat his back.

"Jesus, kid. Warn a guy." A deep, croaky chuckle tag teams his cough. "But I absolutely would have. It's going to take a hell of a man who's good enough for my kid."

And that's my cue.

"About that."

The widening of his eyes shouldn't be comical, but it's hard to contain the panic in his expression. "For the love of god, please don't tell me it's Tyron."

"What?" I barely get the word out, snorting out a

laugh so hard it hurts the back of my throat. "No." I shake my head, still laughing.

"Thank Christ." He wipes a hand over his face. "The kid can carry out a crossover dribble like the best, but away games are about as much as I can handle. Not sure how long either of us would last over family dinners."

A giant, shit-eating, relieved-as-hell grin is plastered on my face.

Since Tyron is one of his players and he's panicking over the guy's ability to press his buttons rather than the fact that he's on the team eases the tightness in my chest. "It's Leon."

Dad looks momentarily startled. "Bradford?"

"Yeah. Leon Bradford's my boyfriend, and I suppose this is me officially telling my supervisor—that'd be you, Coach. As long as I'm not involved in any decision-making that could be misconstrued as favoritism, I promise not to allow my relationship to impact my role."

Dad's silent, listening intently. With the way his eyebrows lift as I speak, it's clear he understands my intention: to take the position he's so graciously offered.

"It could potentially put you under the microscope," I admit with a wince. "But there it is. I like him a lot and want my parents to meet him." At

Dad's bemused expression, I chuckle. "As my dad, not his coach."

"Well, shit." A long pull of his beer later, Dad turns fully toward me. "So today's session, none of that's going to happen on my court again, right?"

Fuck. He's so right. And I'm not even surprised he noticed my odd behavior.

I stand up straighter and look him in the eyes. "I promise that will never happen again, Coach. You have my word."

He huffs out a breath. "Well, that's that, then. I suppose you better go and tell your mom we need to prepare for a guest tomorrow evening for dinner."

"A what now?"

Dad shakes his head and claps me on my back. "Leon's a good kid. A great player. But tomorrow I want to meet your boyfriend and make sure he's good enough for my boy."

I blanch, knowing not to question him. Sure, he's having fun with this, but he's deadly serious. Earlier when I mentioned that protective streak... yeah, not a lie.

"O-kay. I'll see if he can make it."

At Dad's quirked brow, I roll my eyes at him. "Do not be an asshole to him, and if he can't make tomorrow, then that's okay. He's got an assignment due to hand in Friday."

"Fine, but get on the phone now. Then if he can, best tell your mom sooner rather than later. Let her get her reaction out of the way. It'll give her time to decompress." His chuckle is loud, and he sounds far too pleased with himself.

Mom is going to go nuts. In the best possible way, which is totally a thing.

As I head toward my room to make my call, I smile. My heart's lighter, yet close to bursting with feels for my dad.

And holy shit, as soon as I've signed the contract, I'm on my way to finally chasing a career I wasn't sure I'd ever have.

# CHAPTER 19

## LEON

WHEN TILLER TOLD ME NOT ONLY HAS HE SPOKEN TO HIS dad but we're heading to theirs for dinner, talk about awkward levels of mindfuck.

I agreed—obviously since I'm just about to pull up outside his house—but holy shit, nerves are tapdancing in my gut.

Last year before the final game of the championship, I'd been shitting a brick. This, me about to have dinner with *Mr.* Maple rather than *Coach* Maple, is a close second to the intensity of tension thrumming through my veins.

A choppy exhale falls past my lips. I shake out my hands as soon as I've parked and closed the door.

I'm kicking myself for not taking up Tiller's offer to collect me.

Hand raised to the door, an undignified squeak

leaves me when the door opens. My breath freezes in my lungs only to escape in a relieved whoosh. Tiller.

"Hey." His gaze roams my face. I have no idea if I'm pale or bright red, but whatever he sees in my expression has him reaching for me. I go willingly. "You doing okay?"

"Uh-huh," I mumble against his neck. I soak in his heat, using the familiar warmth to calm me.

"Sounds like it." I hear the humor in his voice, but he doesn't outright laugh at me. He knows this is a big deal. "Come on. They're waiting."

That gets me moving and almost falling on my ass with the speed I jerk myself out of his arms.

At his lips twitching, I narrow my gaze. In response, he takes my hand, squeezes lightly, and whispers close to my ear, "It'll be fine. Mom will love you."

I bob my head, more than aware he hasn't mentioned his dad.

Sure, Tiller said Coach took everything in his stride, but this whole situation is beyond daunting.

Taking one foot in front of the other, I follow his lead. I don't doubt he can feel my sweaty palms, but I'm relieved he doesn't mention it. We step into a large open-plan kitchen area. It's modern and bright, though still has a homey feel. Off to the side is a huge space with a large table.

I've been here before, every year in fact for Coach's preseason barbecue, but this is so different to the other times. Then we use the back gate and take over his large patio and expanse of yard. It means I've met Mrs. Maple before, but never more than a "hello" and a "thanks for having us."

"Mom, Dad, Leon's here."

I loosen my fingers, but Tiller's not having any of it. His grip is firm, and I take it as he intended, as a comfort and reassurance.

Coach is standing on the other side of the long countertop, apron on, and a chopping board before him. With folded arms, he's sporting a hard look. Not quite a scowl, but it's enough to let me know he's welcomed me into his home and I best not screw this up.

"Coach." I bob my head and quickly focus on his wife. "Mrs. Maple, thanks for inviting me."

Tiller's mom grins widely. She's a good head shorter than her husband, too, making me wonder exactly where Tiller got his height from. Not that Coach is short, but at maybe five ten, compared to almost all his team, it's no wonder he's perfected his take-no-shit stare.

"It's so wonderful you came." She steps from around the countertop and reaches out for my hand. I drop Tiller's and reach out. Her grip is firm, and while I already knew she was a good woman, between her handshake and the genuine, happy interest in her gaze, I think she's going to be super easy to like.

"Tiller, why don't you organize drinks." She pecks a kiss to his cheek, and I don't miss the way she squeezes his arm, or the even bigger smile she shoots him.

"Absolutely. Beer?" He turns to me, and I hesitate. This is not only Coach's house, but his parents. I need to make a good impression. "A Coke would be great, please."

Again, there's a twitch of his lips, but he doesn't call me out. "Sure thing. Dad?" he asks, turning to Coach who's studying my interaction with his son carefully.

"Beer would be good."

And then I'm standing here, wondering what to do with my hands and wondering how to ease this crazy tension.

When Mrs. Maple says, "Come and perch yourself on a stool while we finish off preparing dinner," I practically fall over my feet, grateful for her save. "How were classes today, Leon?"

Okay, a safe topic. I can handle this.

"Good thanks, Mrs. Maple."

The uptick of her lips is similar to Tiller's and settles something in my chest. "Please, call me—"

"Mrs. Maple will do just fine," Coach interrupts.

Mrs. Maple tuts and openly rolls her eyes at her husband. "If you're going to be ridiculous, you can eat by yourself in the den."

"What? But—"

"But nothing." She shakes her head and gives Coach a look that's filled with magic or mind control or something. I swear he transforms. My mind struggles to catch up, not seeing Coach like this before.

A smile, all weirdly sweet and chipper, appears on his usually scowling face. He steps behind his wife, wrapping his arms around her and kisses her cheek.

I'm staring. I know it. But I can't look away.

Sure, of course he's like this with his wife, but still, it doesn't compute.

As he whispers something that makes her blush, my jaw unhinges, and it's only Tiller reaching my side, chuckling softly as he presses a kiss on top of my head that has me dragging my gaze away.

"Your Coke."

I angle my head to see him as he steps to my side, his gaze soft and amused.

"You sure you don't want a beer?" While he's

teasing, I see the evidence of unspoken concern in the way he's looking at me.

"No," I say, finding my voice. "This is great for now. Maybe after dinner?"

"So classes." Coach's voice has me snapping my attention to him. He's no longer sending me a death stare, which is something. "You were saying?"

"Sure, yeah. Good thanks, Coach. I'm working hard at getting ahead to take the pressure off when season starts."

He bobs his head at that. "Good idea. Balance can be hard."

"It can be, but I've always managed. This year I'll be pulling out all the stops. I need to do as well as possible, this being my last year and all."

"And what is it you're hoping to do after school?" Mrs. Maple asks.

"Project managing."

Mrs. Maple offers me a kind smile. "In a particular sector?"

"Engineering. My dad's an engineer back home, and I always kind of enjoyed watching him work, seeing what he did. Not that I ever wanted to be an engineer, though." I chuckle. "Dad's always been handy, so I can hold my own around a house and a yard, but I've never wanted to do physical work really. The business side, well, the organizational side of things is where I can see myself." I flick my gaze at Coach. While his gaze is unwavering, he's nodding, clearly listening intently.

"It's good that you have a clear pathway," he says. "And where will you plan to settle?"

I go bug-eyed and snap my attention to Tiller. I'm not sure what I'm asking him exactly, what I want him to do or say, but with the way he's peering at me, that soft smile of his already directed my way, I stop panicking.

"I'm not quite sure yet, Coach. I've got plenty of time to apply, but as to where I'll be, there's things I'll need to consider."

Tiller's hand presses on my back, his touch comforting and knowing.

Yeah, I imagine it's pretty damn clear to everyone that I want to see where Tiller ends up. If this season goes well for him, it'll potentially open up so many doors for him. That is if coaching is it for him. I expect it is.

"I'm sure you'll figure it all out when the time comes." Mrs. Maple offers me a smile before she moves to the oven.

"Talking of the future, have you both decided how to handle this?" Coach darts his finger to his son and then me.

I bob my head and look at Tiller. We've talked this through.

"Yeah. We're keeping our relationship on the down-low but are absolutely not hiding it." Tiller's palm snakes up to my neck where he stops and brushes his thumb over my skin.

"Which means what exactly?"

Tiller answers his dad, saying, "We'll maintain professionalism when on the court, in the locker room—"

I snap my attention to Coach when he interrupts with a snort.

"Because you've been doing a stellar job at that."

Holy shit. Fire burns my cheeks. Does that mean he suspected?

"Whatever, Dad, you near enough had a heart attack when you thought I was going to say I was dating Tyron."

A snorting laugh bursts out of me, even as Coach narrows his gaze at his son.

"Ty, really? But he's with—"

"Yes, yes." Coach waves me off. "Call it a combination of my panic and worst nightmare slamming together."

"Really," Mrs. Maple reprimands. "Tyron is a lovely boy."

"I'm not saying he's not a good kid," Coach says

quickly, appeasing his wife. "All I'm actually trying to say is that if yesterday's training is anything to go by, you're going to have to do a better job. While I didn't know you were together, it was clear there was something going on."

I throw Tiller a smirk. That was totally—okay *mainly*—on him.

"Yeah, yeah. I know I was a jerk." When he follows up with a kiss on my temple, my breath catches, and fresh heat burns my cheeks. His mom's soft sigh just makes them scorch hotter. "And yes, we will do a better job," he says to his dad. "Leon's housemates now know, so that's quite a few members of the team, and if we're outright asked, we won't deny our relationship. If we're out eating or at the movie theater, or whatever, I want everyone to know Leon's my boyfriend."

The way my heart gallops in my chest is a worry. I'm sure to god everyone can hear it. But fuck, he's so damn sweet and perfect.

"Jesus H. Christ." Coach is wide-eyed as his gaze darts between the two of us. "So I suppose this is absolutely official, then."

Tiller's "It sure is, Dad," precedes him taking hold of my hand.

"Well, okay then. Before we sit down to eat, I suppose now is the time to say, Bradford, you break my kid's heart and you'll face a feat worse than defeat on the court. By the time I'm done with you, you'll beg for mer—"

"Dad!"

"Seriously, Todd."

I swallow and whisper to Tiller, "I think I'll have that beer now."

Dinner wasn't terrible. Well, the meal was actually amazing, but I don't think I untensed my shoulders the whole time. Talk about awkward. But still, Mrs. Maple went easy on me, and Tiller made sure to fill in any gaps, usually from my side-eyes and not knowing how to behave toward Coach when he's in clear dad mode.

"And do you get to see your parents often?" Mrs. Maple smiles kindly at me. We're sitting outside on the patio taking in the lowering sun. Tiller's at my side, his thigh touching mine, going a long way at helping to keep me at ease.

I'm still nursing my beer, weirdly uncomfortable drinking in front of Coach. Legal or not, it feels odd.

"Not as much as I like. We talk on the phone every week, though."

Coach is in the wicker armchair, not quite opposite me. It helps to stop this from feeling like an inquisition.

"That's good. I know when Tiller traveled those weekly calls meant everything."

Tiller shifts a little at my side, drawing my attention. He's smiling at his mom. "They meant a lot to me, too, Mom."

Mrs. Maple grins, while I smile, liking that Tiller's close to his parents.

"And when are you able to see them? I know Todd keeps you all busy." She glances at her husband.

"Thanksgiving is the plan. It's only a few hours' drive."

"Just north of Nashville did you say?"

"Yes, ma'am."

"And siblings?"

"Mom, you looking at writing a biography? What's with all the questions?" Tiller asks.

I chuckle lightly as his mom narrows her gaze at him. "I'm allowed to get to know your boyfriend better." She peers at me. "I'm sorry if I'm being pushy, but you're the first boyfriend Tiller's ever brought home."

"Not a problem, ma'am. I don't mind. And yes, I have two younger sisters. One's at college in Chicago. One's still in high school."

"And have you ever taken a boyfriend home for your parents to meet?"

"Mom, seriously." Tiller turns to look at me. "You don't have to answer that."

At his worry as well as his attempt at defending me, warmth fizzes in my stomach. "It's okay," I say softly. Turning back, I focus first on Coach, who's watching me with unhidden interest, then look at Mrs. Maple. "No, ma'am, I haven't. I had a girlfriend back in high school, who met my parents, but no boyfriend until Tiller, and I definitely want them to meet him."

Tiller's soft "You do?" pulls my attention immediately to him.

"Of course I do. I was actually going to ask if you wanted to come home with me at Thanksgiving."

The small smile playing on his lips widens. The fizz in my stomach goes crazy, loving that such happiness is directed my way.

"You don't mind? You don't need to talk to them by yourself?"

"I want you there. My parents will love you."

The pink in his cheeks has me barely holding back my happy sigh.

"Yeah, okay. I'd love to."

Coach clearing his throat has us jerking our attention in his direction. While he doesn't look pissed off, he is looking pointedly at Tiller before darting a quick gaze at his wife.

"Shit, Mom, do you mind? I know it's my first Thanksgiving home in—"

"Five years," his mom finishes for him. The soft smile she shoots him is reassuring, at least. Not that I don't feel guilty for trying to steal him away. Like me, I imagine Tiller rarely got home for any holiday. A college basketball player is tied to the game schedule.

"Uhm… sorry, I didn't think. That's okay. You should be here with your parents." While I say the words and mean them, it doesn't stop the sinking in my gut.

I'm not exactly worried about telling my parents about having a boyfriend, but I'm admittedly nervous. Having Tiller by my side would mean a whole lot and go a long way toward building my confidence.

A concerned frown mars Tiller's face. "But telling your parents…," he all but whispers. He doesn't say any more, and I appreciate that since we have an audience.

Not that I mind.

"Honestly, it's fine. I've already told you they'll be okay."

I believe it. I do. Though that doesn't stop that

niggling nervousness from bouncing around in my chest.

"Leon, son." I jolt at Coach's voice. It's far from stern, but the use of "son" completely throws me. I face him immediately, used to reacting to his requests and instructions without delay.

There's a frown, pretty identical to his son's, on his face.

"You don't have to answer, but do your parents know you date men? Is that the reason you've never taken a boyfriend home before?"

"No, sir, they do not," I answer honestly, trying to ignore how awkward this whole conversation is. But Coach is a good guy. I know he's always looking out for my and every other player's best interests. Then there's his son, who he loves fiercely.

I don't need the knowledge Tiller's shared with me to make that clear.

"Todd."

Coach looks at his wife. There's this whole wordless exchange that only couples who've been together forever have. My parents can have a whole conversation like this.

"I think you having Thanksgiving in Nashville will be wonderful, Tiller. It means we get you both at Christmas. No doubt you'll all be away for a game on the twenty-sixth, so it's almost impossible for anyone to go home. This works out perfectly."

It's official. Mrs. Maple is awesome. Not only can she make a kick-ass pot roast, but she's letting me keep Tiller, and giving me an invite for Christmas.

It's not hard to see why Tiller turned out to be so incredible.

I'm smiling, heart full, as Tiller takes hold of my hand. His gaze is on his parents as he says, "Thanks, Mom, Dad. That all sounds great."

Squeezing his hand, I bob my head. "Thanks, Mrs. Maple, Coach. I appreciate the invite."

Coach nods once, and his shoulders fully relax.

Holy shit, this feels pretty much like I've been accepted into the family.

Sure, my mind's a little boggled by the events, but I've gotta admit, I like it a helluva lot.

***

WATER SLUICES OVER MY FACE, MY HEAD, THEN OVER MY back. "I don't have the energy to move."

Sammy's snort from the neighboring shower reaches me. "Those last thirty seconds on the clock..." He sighs and a loud, albeit tired moan follows. "Not sure how I made it. Yo, Bentley, how's your back?"

"What? Why?" Suspicion fills his questions.

"Dibs on a piggyback on the way home."

A chorus of laughter and snorts fills the space at Sammy's words.

"Keep dreaming, Sammy," Benny calls out, amusement coloring his tone.

I switch off the water, wrap myself in my towel, and step out of the shower cubicle. There's a shake in my legs, a testimony to just how hard we were pushed tonight. Thank Christ we have a training-free day tomorrow. Just the thought of running or doing any type of exercise in the next twenty-fours is enough to make me grimace.

Dropping down heavily on the bench in front of my cubby, I build up the will to grab my gear so I can dress and get out of here.

"What's the matter, Bradford? Can't hack the drills?"

It's a struggle to hold back my sigh at Jones's bitchiness. The guy tries to get a dig in whenever possible. It's best to ignore him, but he's relentless in his ability to be a cockhead.

"Just worry about yourself, Jones." I don't even look in his direction as I speak. No doubt his spiteful brown eyes are speared my way as he fantasizes about all the ways he can knock me out of the starting five.

"Whatever, man. Perhaps you're pushing yourself too hard. Just looking out for you, is all."

I can't not look at him. He's so full of shit. "What, you're worried about me? Aw, Jones. I'm flattered. I didn't know you cared."

A tightness appears around his eyes, but his lips are curved up. "Of course I care, Bradford. You've kept my spot warm on the starting line all this time. I appreciate it."

Sammy's snort cuts me short from telling him to go fuck himself.

"Damn, Jones. You ever heard of playing hard to get? Pulling your junk out for us all to see is a bit crass, don't ya think? Next you're going to be asking for a measuring stick." He pauses, stopping before Jones just in his towel. He pinches his chin as though deep in thought. "Maybe they do those tiny rulers you get in those math kits when at school. They're only, what, four inches, right? That's more than big enough if you want to keep measuring your cock."

I clamp my mouth shut to stop from barking out my laugh. It's oh so tempting, especially when Sammy heads to his cubby snickering, but Jones's expression has turned thunderous. Me joining him is likely to push him over the edge, and no way am I letting his jealousy interfere with my position on the team.

Plus, having Coach pissed off at me? Hell no.

Even before I started dating his son, I avoided annoying or disappointing him. Now? No chance I want to rock that boat.

Jones is strangely quiet after Sammy's verbal slamming. If he could shoot lasers out of his eyes, Sammy would be vaporized. His jaw ticks, and then his gaze is on me. A sneer forms as he stands.

I tense, muscles vibrating when he takes a few steps toward the exit, which is also in my direction. He stops less than an arm's length from me, peering down.

Forcing myself to relax, I quirk my eyebrow.

This kid has some serious issues. And if he expects he's got a hope in hell of intimidating me, he's got another think coming.

"Always someone around to do the hard work for you, Bradford." His lips twist. "Sounds about right."

"Jones." Kieran's voice is hard. "A word."

A humorless snort escapes Jones. "And there it is." He peers over his shoulder, gaze moving to his captain. When Kieran indicates for him to leave and takes a step in our direction, Jones bobs his head. "Sure thing, Cap."

Without another word, he leaves, Kieran close on his heels. As he passes me, Kieran glances my way, the unspoken question easy for me to read.

"No idea what the fuck his problem is." I shrug, acting more carefree than I really feel.

While my shoulders are still relaxed, the asshole got under my skin and set my teeth on edge. The fuck is wrong with the guy?

"Jesus," Sammy says loudly, following up with a low whistle when Jones and Kieran have exited the locker room. "Think he's having his time of the month. Maybe we need to buy him some jerky or something." I look his way, noticing everyone had clearly watched that whole exchange. Though Sammy's words earn a few snickers, helping to cut through the tension.

Confusion still remains on all but two expressions.

The first is Sammy, who apparently lives for the drama.

Then there's Tyron. Legs parted, feet firmly on the tiled floor, he's a wall of intense muscle. His arms are folded, expression even more stoic than normal. He's watching the exit.

That is until his gaze travels to me. An up-nod follows. *Am I okay?* I return the gesture, offering a slight twitch of my lips.

Seemingly satisfied with my response, he turns away from me and the exit and focuses on dressing.

Taking calming breaths, I take stock of the

exchange and my friends having my back. Whatever Jones's problem is, I hope he gets over himself sooner rather than later. Whenever he's around, there's an undeniable strain in the team.

None of us want to deal with that bullshit.

Feeling calmer, I dress, thinking instead about spending the night with Tiller.

Since coming out to my housemates and disclosing our relationship to Coach, life's so much sweeter. And a whole lot less stressful.

Tiller staying the night regularly is a huge bonus too.

Since he's part of the reason for my overworked muscles during practice, maybe I can guilt him into a massage. Amused, knowing it won't take too much convincing, I gather my things and wait impatiently for my housemates to finish up so I can get my boyfriend to lather me with attention.

# CHAPTER 20

## TILLER

Two weeks into my new official position, and it's a struggle not to pinch myself.

Sure, I went through some shit to get here, but it's all worth it.

To be training, learning from the best while imparting my knowledge on the team, all while spending my free time with Leon, and yeah, still picking up a couple of shifts at the coffee shop, is pretty damn perfect.

"You about ready?"

Leon turns to me, his T-shirt in his hands and a smirk on his face. "You want me to go shirtless, huh?"

I roll my eyes and remain leaning back, bracing my hands on his mattress. "The view's pretty nice."

His gaze roams my covered chest. "Maybe, but

not as nice as the one I know is hiding under that Iron Maiden tee." Leon's made it no secret that he loves my ink. Or my piercings either. He's spent countless hours tracing my tattoos with his fingers, sometimes with his tongue, and on special occasions when he's feeling extra horny, with his cock too. Those are by far my favorite times.

"You ever think about getting any?"

He tenses his muscles, puffing out his chest a little. I chuckle at his display. "What, and blemish all of this perfect, untouched skin?"

"It is pretty perfect." Heat pools in my stomach as I take him in. "You want to come over here and I can show you how perfect I think your skin is?"

He drops his T-shirt and prowls toward me, a playful, heated glint in his eyes.

I love it when he's like this, all hot and needy. Admittedly, I love every version of him. It's something I try to communicate every time we touch. Every time my gaze rakes over his body or we share a quiet conversation.

I plan to tell him, too, but each time I consider saying the words, I swallow them back. Partly I'm worried about them sounding forced, or too contrived. Don't get me wrong, even to my ears I know how ridiculous that sounds. I didn't say my reasoning made sense.

It's also maybe a little to do with me waiting for the bubble to burst.

The last thing I want to do is compare what we have to what I had with Curtis. Leon's nothing like him. That, and we're out. My parents, the coaches, and his housemates know. We're not sharing it wildly. Not making a grand announcement to the team.

One, because there's no need, and two, because it's our private business. But we're not keeping it a secret either.

On the court, I'm professional and treating Leon like any other player. It's tricky but doable. I'm friendly. We laugh and joke. I'm not keeping my distance. But nor am I rubbing up and down him or kissing him hello.

If we're out holding hands or making out in the back of a movie theater, then again, that's our business too.

"What's with the serious expression?"

I snap out of my thoughts and clamp my hands on his waist, tugging him the few inches closer from where he'd stopped in concern apparently. "It's your fault," I tease. "You get me so distracted that my brain misfires every now and then."

He snorts and pushes me, straddling my waist as my back hits the mattress. "You're so full of shit, but if you want to keep talking about how perfect I am, have right at it."

Pausing the trail of my fingers over his thighs, I quirk my eyebrow. "I thought I said perfect *skin*?"

"To-may-to, to-mah-to."

Snagging him in a gentle hold, I haul him down and capture his mouth. He opens immediately, accepting my tongue, kissing me slowly as he shifts his hips so his jean-clad cock rubs over mine.

There's no holding back the groan.

"You think there's enough time for you to put your dick in my mouth bef—"

"Knock, knock, assholes." A heavy thud punctuates the words, and I moan in defeat, pressing my head against the mattress. "We're leaving."

"Has he always been a cockblocker?" I ask.

"Yeah, but I get my own back when I see him sneak away into his room. Ty is not as stealth as he thinks he is." With one last push of his hips, Leon jumps off me, leaving me with a hard dick and a bulge in my jeans that's going to be difficult to disguise.

"Really?" I stare pointedly at my bulge, then at Leon.

"Just something to think about before you crawl under me... or over me tonight?"

I reach out for a pillow and throw it, getting a

little satisfaction when it hits Leon in the face. The bastard laughs. "What is it about a team barbecue at my parents' house that makes you think telling me that is a good idea?" I shake my head as I sit up, adjusting my dick as I do so. "Dude, that's seriously dark."

Since Leon's still laughing while tugging his T-shirt on, he apparently thinks he's hilarious. I narrow my gaze at him as I stand and step into his space, a smirk forming on my mouth. At the movement, Leon's lips twitch.

"You know two can play that game, right?"

Leon's widening eyes have amusement dancing over my skin.

"Meaning what, exactly?"

Oh, he's so going to get it. "Don't worry that perfect head of yours. Come on. Let's get going. Can't be tardy unless you want Dad adding time to the clock next practice."

There's a scowl on his face, but humor lights up his gaze. Instead of pushing, he presses his mouth to mine, kissing me tenderly. As he pulls away, just far enough for our eyes to connect, he smirks, saying, "Bring it, baby."

Oh, it's on.

The whole team and basketball staff are here. Dad's manning the grill, Mom's kicking back on the outdoor suite, accepting the team pretty much waiting on her while happily sipping wine and talking to Burt's wife, Lisa, and I'm wondering how I can mess with Leon.

We've been apart most of the evening. Not necessarily a problem since I managed to spend a couple of quality of hours with him today. Plus, it's hard not to get handsy.

We're definitely not keeping our relationship a secret. Far from it. But even though we're at my home, this is still a work event of sorts, which means while I have a beer in hand, I'm not glugging it like water, and I'm going to stay mostly professional.

Because yeah, back to wanting to mess with my boyfriend.

He's laughing loudly at something Dean, our mascot and Kieran's boyfriend, is saying. It's hard to look away when he's so relaxed, but Mom asked me to get the tray of desserts out of the refrigerator, so I need to haul ass.

"You need a hand?"

I pull my attention away from Leon and hesitate to step through the patio door through to the kitchen. My gaze lands on a smiling Gavin Jones. "Yeah, sure. Just grabbing a couple of trays of desserts."

I haven't spent much time talking to Jones outside of practice.

He's got a lot of potential, but I know he's earned the wrath of Dad a couple of times, mainly as he's not been fully focused. That's one major way of frustrating Dad.

He expects commitment and dedication. Sure, he'll give a free pass if there's a legit reason, but I'm not aware of anything going on in Jones's life that is a cause for his distraction.

"You having a good night?" I ask, stepping into our large kitchen.

"Yeah. Coach knows how to grill."

I chuckle and flick my gaze in his direction as we reach the fridge. "He does that." Tugging open the door, I easily find a tray of desserts and carefully pull it out before passing it to Jones. "And how's everything at school? I remember the first few months can be a little rough, especially finding the balance between assignments and training... and all the freedom of living away from home." I pull the second tray out and push the door closed with my hip.

"It's been an adjustment, but I'm coping."

"That's good." I bob my head.

The kid's only eighteen and has the whole preppy jock look going on. His expression is open, attentive, and I can't help but wonder if he's being completely honest with me or himself about how well he's settling in.

"And how about the team? You finding your place?" I place the tray on the countertop, giving Jones my full attention.

There's a shift in his expression, and his smile loses some of its shine. "Yeah, I guess."

"You guess?"

At my furrowed brow, he shrugs. "It's hard when the team's so well-established."

Understanding what he means, I nod and offer a sympathetic smile. "I see that, especially when you're dealing with a championship team." I don't need to add that five key members of the team are best friends and housemates. "It'll get easier. You follow Coach's instructions, train hard, and keep focused, I'm sure you'll get your shot."

If he does, I expect he'll be a shoo-in for the starting five next season. With Leon leaving—hell, so many of the team graduating—there's lots of spots opening.

But as a shooting guard, I know he's chasing Leon's spot.

"You think?"

"I know it."

A more genuine smile lifts his lips. "How about this season?"

I chuckle and shake my head. "Now that's all down to Coach and to you. You need to give Coach a reason to give you a shot. Make it clear you deserve game time and should be on the bench all game."

"If only I knew an assistant coach who had the ear of Coach Maple." There's a teasing glint in his eyes.

A snorting laugh escapes me. "Ha. One thing you need to know about Coach is this is very much his team."

Nodding, Jones is still smiling. "I hear you. Maybe I'll talk to Coach about getting in on the one-on-one action you've been dedicating to Bradford."

The smile freezes on my face, and unease shifts in my chest. Keeping my expression the same, I shrug. "That's something you can chat with him about. Coach has complete control over where he wants me to spend my time in training. I don't get to pick and choose."

"Yeah, that makes sense." A twist of his lips and the dip of his brow alert me to his discomfort. "I don't suppose you offer private training sessions or anything." He rubs his spare hand over the back of his head, his expression turning sheepish. "I may have spent some time going over your game footage."

Surprise slams into me, and my eyebrows shoot up. "Oh wow… really?" An awkward laugh slips out of me. "Damn, there's a lot more impressive players to spend your time studying."

"I'm not sure about that. That Philly game." Wide-eyed, he stares at me. "Now *that* was impressive as hell."

Embarrassed at his attention and hoping like hell he's just being a fan and not flirting, I clear my throat. "Well, thanks. It was a good game. Our team was on fire." I focus on the tray, wanting to escape. Picking it up, I indicate over my shoulder with a head flick. "Mom's going to be wondering where I got to."

"Yeah, sure, of course."

Stepping away, I head toward the patio door. The slightly cooler air hits me. It's refreshing and welcome after the awkwardness of the last couple of minutes.

"Just over here," I instruct Jones, placing my tray on the table.

He sets his down and looks my way. "Will you think about the training?"

"I don't really have time for private coaching," I settle on.

Tightness forms around his eyes. It's there for just

a second before it disappears. "Sure, no problem. Thought it was worth an ask. I'll definitely talk to Coach, though."

"You do that." I bob my head and look for my escape. Leon's eyes are lasered on me. I search his gaze, wondering what he's thinking. "I'll catch you later, Jones. Have a good night." I barely cast him a look, too eager to get to Leon.

In a few short strides I finally reach his side. Bentley gives me an up-nod before he focuses on something Sammy is saying.

"I just brought out dessert. You don't want to miss Mom's mini cheesecakes." I bounce my brows up and down for good measure. A slither of a smile appears, but it's tighter than normal and doesn't reach his eyes. I lower my voice, asking, "You okay?"

"Yeah." His eyes widen, and he seems to shake off whatever was bothering him, a wider smile forming. "I'm always down for cheesecake. You want to lead the way?"

"Right this way."

No idea what that was about. Maybe he's just as keen as I am to get out of here and finish what we started before we were dragged away by Tyron.

We stop at the table and I swipe a cheesecake, shoving it unceremoniously into my mouth. I turn in Leon's direction, my cheeks puffed out. Once again I bob my eyebrows up and down. This time it earns me a laugh.

"That good, huh?"

I'm nodding as I chew. When I've emptied my mouth, I lean in a fraction. "Second best thing I'll have in my mouth today."

Heat flares in his eyes, just as I hoped. Roaming his face, I dip my gaze to the column of his throat, enjoying the heavy gulp that follows. My dick twinges, but that's okay. I'm pretty sure he's gone from soft to steel. The temptation to let my attention dip lower is there, but since my dad is standing in my periphery, I best not.

That doesn't mean I can't make good on my promise and pay him back for the hard-on he gave me before we came here tonight.

"You know," I continue, my lips deliberately brushing his ear, "I've yet to truly swallow your cock, feel it wedged in my throat." The hitch in his breath is the best sound I've heard all night. "I best get another drink to make sure my throat isn't dry if we can make that happen later."

As I pull away, we make eye contact. His pupils are blown, and his cheeks are tinged pink. The heavy breathing falling from his lips urges me on to capture them. Instead, I back away, fully aware my cock's hard.

There's nothing I can do about that, though. Well, not now.

"You want anything?"

At my question, his gaze narrows. It's the twitching of his lips that draws my attention, though. "A Coke. Best I keep sober." The quirk of his eyebrow is all sass, and fuck if I don't love it.

"Good plan." A shoot him a wink before turning and heading to get us drinks. Noticing Jones's focus on me, I smile at him. It's brighter than I intended, but with Leon's reaction making my thoughts fuzzy, it's hard to hold back my happy buzz.

I wonder how long I need to hold out before I can steal Leon away.

Another hour at least, I expect. I just need to keep it together until then and not be tempted to drag him into my bedroom.

***

IT TAKES SO MUCH LONGER THAN AN HOUR. I COULDN'T ditch Mom or Dad, leaving them with the cleanup. Between me, Leon, and his housemates, who offered to stay back and help out, we get back to Leon's about three hours later than I planned.

"Are you tired?"

In answer, I step up behind Leon as he's reaching

to open his bedroom door and press a kiss against his mouth. He sighs into the touch and allows me to cling on as we move inside.

Not stepping away from the trail of kisses I dot along his neck, I reach blindly to lock his door. At the snick of the catch, Leon chuckles.

"That'll be a not tired, then, huh?"

I run a hand down his stomach and grip his hardening dick. "That'll be a hell no. I promised you something."

A grunt tears from his lips, and I squeeze his junk again.

"Get naked and on the bed. The sooner you do, the soone—"

My arms are empty as he all but dives away, tugging his clothes off frantically.

With a mischievous grin, I pull my tee off, my gaze unwavering as he strips.

By the time I'm stepping out of my jeans, he's naked on the bed, his hand working his cock.

The need firing through my belly is one way to get me moving. I'm on him, wiping away his sultry smile with a searing kiss.

Clamping his hands to my back, he eagerly holds on, and fuck if I don't surrender to the pleasure of his lips on mine. I'm so hard, this kiss so perfect, it won't take much for me to explode.

It's tempting. But the promise of deep-throating him is one I don't want to ignore. Not after his reaction at the team barbecue. As I trail my lips down his neck, a delicious tremor ripples through him, sending jolts of awareness across my skin.

There's no time for hesitation or delay. Not when with each panted breath I feel his need. I focus on the pulsing heat between us. On the ache I just know he's feeling the longer I delay wrapping my lips around him. With the determination of a talent scout seeking the next big thing, my mouth finds his cock, engulfing his head.

"Oh fuck," he blurts, his voice laced with a mixture of disbelief and ecstasy as I take him deeper.

A low, primal growl escapes my throat, causing him to clench and gasp. Even with the mattress beneath me and Leon filling all my senses, I feel untethered. His pleasure, his vibrating body and needy gasps are enough to have me clinging on for dear life, trying not to float away or come undone.

Tilting his head back, Leon surrenders completely. To wetness that coats his shaft, the fiery suction—it consumes him entirely. And fuck if he's not everything in this moment.

He's heavy on my tongue and thick in my mouth.

As I tighten my grip at the base of his cock, his gaze snaps downward. The craving I see in it spurs me on. With my eyes on his, I release my hand and take more of him, as much as I can.

I relax my throat and his eyes widen, his mouth forming an *O*.

"Fuck, that's… that's…," he gasps, his voice filled with awe. It's enough to make me keep going.

I close my eyes, pull back up, inhale deeply, then suck him into my mouth.

The nudge of his cock in my throat has my limbs shaking and his body tensing.

More. I need everything.

I swallow. Once. Twice.

A strangled moan rips from him, and I pull away, gasping.

Eyes now open, our gazes lock. He's frozen, ensnared, and so close to blowing, his cock pulsing.

With unwavering determination, I suck him long and slow. Savoring the anticipation that dances between us, I don't look away. My throat is sore, and I expect I'm going to sound gruff as hell, but this, his tender expression, his open need, it's worth it.

Leon bites his lip, a silent plea for more. My focus dances from his mouth to his eyes, conveying a promise. *I've got you.* And then, with a torturous slowness that threatens to unravel us both, I press forward, swallowing him whole until I gag. And holy fuck, he hardens even more.

Not giving up, I continue my descent, taking him deep into my throat.

I hold him there, relishing in the rawness of the moment, feeling the tremor as he struggles to hold still.

"Oh holy… nngh." He releases directly in my throat.

My world tilts, pleasure rippling through me. I pull back gasping, needing oxygen.

His cum pulses out of him. I lean back down and lap it up, savoring not only his taste but the shuddering gasp escaping him.

"You okay?"

Fuck, my throat's rough. Hell if I don't smirk at the sound.

"Holy shit, Tiller." With his eyelids at half-mast, Leon looks thoroughly fucked. He lazily shakes his head, forearm on his forehead as he inhales a deep breath. "That…." Another shaky breath follows. "How the fuck did you do that?"

At his praise, warmth fills my chest. A satisfied grin follows. "You liked it."

"Fuck no." His eyes spring wide. "I fucking loved it. Jesus. I don't think I've ever come so hard."

Amused, I crawl up his body and lean over him. "That right?" I challenge. "What about when…?"

Fresh pink appears on his cheeks. "Okay, second hardest." A sweet smile follows.

A grunt pushes out of me when he wraps his arms around me and tugs me close. It's a good thing he's pretty much the same size as me and I know he can handle my weight. I smile into his hug, basking in the affection, welcoming the surge of emotion flooding my heart.

"Give me a minute and I'm so going to try that on you."

I chuckle against his neck, not missing the exhaustion in his voice.

"How about we sleep and we see what the morning brings?"

He leans away, lifting his head so he can make eye contact. "Don't you need to…?" He trails off, his eyebrows shooting high.

"That'll be a no, and we probably need to change your sheets."

Fuck if I don't love the surprise morphing his features. And when his expression shifts into one of complete satisfaction, I love that just as much.

"That is so hot."

I chuckle and capture a sweet kiss from him. "I'm pleased you think me coming without as much as jacking myself off is a good thing."

The tenderest of smiles settles on his mouth as his

gaze roams my face. "I think you coming because I came and clearly loved every single thing you did to me is the best compliment ever."

The sincerity in his words has my heart stumbling before it seems to swell in size with how much I feel for this man. Not sure I can speak without my voice shaking, I let him know just how his words impact me by stealing a kiss and making him breathless all over again.

# CHAPTER 21

## LEON

This is the third training session that Coach has asked Tiller to spend some time with Jones. Tiller's at the other end of the court where I'm meant to be running through some shooting drills.

Ty and a couple of the other guys are doing the same, but my attention is so shit, I'm going to get Coach's attention on me for all the wrong reasons if I don't sort my head out.

"He asked Coach Maple to work with Tiller on decision-making drills."

Startled, I jerk at Ty's words. Not realizing he'd stopped at my side, it takes me a moment for my brain to catch up with his words. "What? Who, Jones?"

There's no point bullshitting Ty about, well,

anything. He's much too smart to even try to outwit him.

"Yeah. You haven't asked Tiller about it?"

I shake my head. "I deliberately don't talk about practice or team stuff. Well, nothing that could make things awkward, you know?"

Since Ty walked us through the nepotism policy, he'll understand my concern.

The last thing I want is for Tiller to feel uncomfortable. Not only that, but he can't play favorites. It's something both of us agreed on before he first spoke to his dad.

It doesn't mean I have to like the extra time he's spending with Jones, though.

"You're not worried, right?"

Making eye contact with Ty, I frown. "About what? Tiller, as in am I jealous?"

Ty shrugs.

Am I? Well, I'd prefer to be spending time with Tiller, but I'm not jealous about him doing his job. "No. That it's Jones gets my back up," I admit.

"Because he's an asshole and is up to something?"

"What?" Panic jolts me. Wide-eyed, I ask, "Up to what? What do you mean?" I don't need to agree to Ty describing Jones as an asshole. We all know he is. While he hasn't shouted any venom in my direction since the last time Kieran took him aside to have a conversation with him, I have no expectation that our captain magicked the jerk out of him.

From all I've seen, he's too obnoxious and self-entitled for him to have a complete about-face.

"Not sure yet."

"Seriously, Ty. You can't just say that."

Ty moves his gaze away from my boyfriend and Jones. "Something's off. We all know he's got grand ambitions, and I expect he's the sort of guy who doesn't give a shit about who he steps on to get what he wants."

Dread curdles my gut. "You think he wants Tiller?"

Ty scrunches his brow. "If you're asking if he has designs on your man"—the asshole quirks his brow, a glimmer of amusement in his eyes—"then no. I don't think he wants to get in his pants."

I roll my eyes, at myself more than Ty. Nothing like feeling like an idiot.

Ty's "But I wouldn't put it past Jones to use Tiller in some way if it'll get him what he wants" has all my humor fading.

Once again, he makes to move. Grabbing his arm, I stop him. "Seriously, dude, stop with the bomb-shells, then trying to swan off."

"Swanning off. Really?" he deadpans.

I wave his sarcasm away and shoot him a hard

stare. All that seems to do is amuse him. Ty has intense stares perfected, so I get it.

"Like I said, I don't know yet, but I promise when I find out, you'll be the first to know."

I'll take it. Ty is nothing if not tenacious.

"Okay, thanks, Ty."

He bobs his head and indicates for me to follow. I do, aware my stopping and staring could get me into shit.

It doesn't make not staring at Tiller any easier, though.

As usual, I'm a tired, sweaty mess after practice.

I drag myself to the locker room to shower. Once I'm done, I'll be heading straight to the library. I have a joint research project due in soon. It means no slacking off, and no getting distracted in Tiller's arms tonight.

I'm contemplating if I'll have the energy to fit in a hot and dirty video call with Tiller later when Jones's laugh slides over me, setting my teeth on edge. It's not a sound I hear often—you know, because he's a complaining jerkoff—but today, it grates.

I try to block out the sound as I step into the small cubicle and turn the shower on. The shower area is tucked away from the main locker room, but it's not isolated. It means sounds can carry, and beyond the cheap shower curtain, there's no real privacy.

Pushing my irritation away, I focus on washing my hair. I'm rinsing the suds out when Davey's voice, one of the other freshmen—a guy who's pretty much blended in with the walls, to be honest—catches my attention.

I tilt my head out of the stream of water, frowning in concentration.

Pockets of words drift toward me. It's the mention of Tiller that has me stepping out of the flow completely, paying closer attention.

"It's true. My cousin Perry went to the same college. Was a sophomore when he'd been a senior. The year after Tiller graduated, there was a shitload of rumors flying around about him."

Fuck no.

I grab my towel and have barely wrapped it around me when I shove aside the flimsy curtain. Two pairs of eyes snap in my direction.

Davey blanches. Jones sneers.

"By all means, don't let me stop you." My feet are planted firmly on the floor, hips' width apart. I fold my arms, wanting to hide my hands. Easy access could get me in a whirlwind of trouble if Jones has the nerve to say something to me.

"Nothing," Davey's quick to say. At my look of disbelief, he stutters, "One of my cousins just knows Assistant Coach Maple, is all."

"And the gossiping bullshit you were so keen to get off your chest, want to share with the rest of us?" Ty steps fully into view from around the corner, and fuck if that isn't perfect timing.

"No." Davey shakes his head. "It's nothing. I shouldn't have said anything."

"No. You shouldn't. Disrespecting one of your coaches like that, and while still here, in the locker room? Get a clue, Davey."

I can't not look at Jones, who's been unusually quiet during this whole exchange.

I'm greeted by a frustratingly impassive expression.

If anything, the fuckhead appears amused, despite not a single twitch of his lips.

"We done here?" The steel in Ty's voice has Davey tensing. The only thing from Jones is a barely there tightening of his eyes.

"Yeah, I'm coming." I eyeball Jones. Why the fuck can't he just snap or something, get himself in more shit?

Instead, he watches me leave, his gaze burning a hole in the back of my head.

Kieran's watching me when I get to my cubby with question in his eyes. I shake my head. I'll talk to him later at home.

The real concern is do I let Tiller know some of the guys are gossiping about him?

Is this one of those times I don't share since it's locker room talk and he's on staff? If someone was saying shit about one of the other coaches, I wouldn't go running to them, letting them know what's being said behind their back.

But this is my boyfriend. The complication is inevitable.

Fuck it all to hell.

Frustrated, I dress, shoving my things into my bag.

For now, I need to concentrate on getting to the library and getting this group task down. I'll think about everything else later.

***

"LATER" IS A SMACK IN MY FACE.

We've had a couple of training sessions, two more nights not spent with Tiller—only snatched conversations and video calls—and it's now, in the gym doing bicep curls, that the smack happens.

"The fuck is this?"

Thunder fills Ty's face. His jaw clenches, and there's a legit creak from how hard he's grinding his teeth.

Rather than answer me, he waits me out, indicating I should read the college post exchange. It's on one of the forums, specifically for bullshit gossip, but the fact that Tiller's image is at the top sends my pulse skyrocketing.

MFran23725: Nothing screams fuckboy more than the clap!!!!!

TLong44532: Makes sense why CM had to get him a job. 🙄

MFran23725: Like eww… I'm gonna need a stick to create a safe space

MFran23725: Heard he's all over the team. Offering to share the love 🤮🤢

TLong44532: I just bet he is. Dirty 💦 😈😎🔥🍑👅👅

BTank76899: 🤣😂

LFork27655: Takes the stickiness of MAPLE to a whole new level… puss 🤮😂🍆💦😳

TLong44532: OMG. DYING!!!!!!!!!

YFran23725: That's not the good stuff coming out of that eggplant. 🤣😂

I've read enough.

I see red.

I also see Jones on his phone, scrolling and wear a huge smirk.

Body tensing, I make to move. A wall of muscles gets in my way.

"The fuck, Ty!" I'm loud enough to get Kieran's and Banks's attention.

"You want me to move so you can… what?"

I fist my hands, limbs trembling. He full well knows I want to get up in Jones's face, ideally with my fist.

Before I can say as much, he continues. "What?" he pushes. "Make sure you get kicked off the team? Lose your scholarship? Give up your spot to the fucker who deserves it the least?"

Air gushes from my lungs as I shake my head.

"In that case, get your shit together. We're leaving." His voice is pitched low, but I'm sure Kieran and Banks can hear at least some of what we're saying.

"We are? But—"

"I'll square it away with Coach," he says, referring to our strength trainer. "Get your ass moving. Don't bother showering. Meet you outside the locker room in ten."

Lead weighs down my feet. Turning away seems

impossible.

"Don't even look at him."

For fuck's sake. I huff out a breath, hating while also being reluctantly grateful Ty can read me so well.

But he's right. If I happen to catch Jones's gaze, I don't think I'll be able to hold back. The thought should terrify me. The last time I had a fight was when I was fifteen, and it was over before it really started.

The need to see that smirk wiped from his face is one hell of a temptation, though.

Still in my space, Ty doesn't relent.

"Yeah, okay. I'm going."

When he still doesn't move, I release a frustrated sigh and walk away, focusing on the floor rather than anyone around me.

It's all I can do to strip out of my sweat-soaked shirt. The adrenaline crash makes my hands shake. By the time I've finally changed and am heading out of the locker room, my head's a little clearer. Calmer.

Fuck. Tiller. This is going to hurt him so fucking bad.

My stomach twists just thinking about his reaction.

Jesus, what if he's already seen it? What if someone's said something to him?

Why the hell is the thread still up there? We need to get that bullshit down.

A fresh wave of anger slices through me.

I'll eat my left fucking nut if this isn't Jones's doing. There's no doubt in my mind, or Ty's apparently, that this has his vicious name all over it.

But to what end? What's he trying to achieve?

Messing with his Coach's son is a surefire way to get him off the team. Surely he knows that, right?

Another couple of minutes pass by, and there's still no Ty. Feeling antsy, I tug out my phone, checking to see if Tiller's reached out to me.

He hasn't.

That's a good thing. At least I'll try to convince myself of that. He has a shift at the coffee shop right now. I check the time—it started just thirty minutes ago. He's working until close, which is eight o'clock tonight.

Hopefully that'll keep him in a protective bubble. Unless some asshole shoves this bullshit in his face while he's at work.

A rush of anger rises to the surface once again.

And where the hell is Ty? Ten minutes, my ass.

Shit. What do I do?

I open my contacts and start typing in Ty's name. The exit door opening draws my attention. Tyron. Thank Christ.

I part my lips, ready to give him shit that his ten minutes is closer to fifteen, but the expression on his face has me pausing. "What is it?" I ask, not sure what to make of the glimmer of satisfaction in his gaze. "I swear if you've kicked Jones's ass without me...."

He scoffs and rolls his eyes. "While he deserves it, no. He's still in the gym, on the treadmill."

"So what, you rigged the treadmill to go kaboom?"

"Not today."

I sigh, but his calm eases some of my tension.

"Come with me."

When Ty's like this, it's easier to not ask questions. So I follow him, our long legs eating up the pavement. A spark of interest pings in my brain when I realize where we're heading, the first hint of a smile trying to break free on my lips.

"Please tell me you're going to do what I think you're going to do." I side-eye Ty, a flip of excitement taking place in my gut when a don't-you-fucking-know-what-a-genius-I-am smirk splits his lips.

I'm not even surprised when Logan greets us at the entryway to the IT lab.

"I got your text. We really doing this?" The flush of Logan's skin makes him look nervous. It's at odds with the sparkle of excitement in his eyes.

"You know it." Ty glances at me. "Logan brought the feed to my attention."

I bob my head, casting a look at Logan. A hardness I'm not used to seeing on his face sets in his features. He's such an easygoing guy, super smart too —I reckon he needs to be to be able to keep up with Ty.

"We'll get his sorted. Tiller doesn't deserve this."

Logan's support settles me even more. "No, he doesn't. Thanks for helping."

Logan nods as we step farther into the building. This isn't an area I really visit. Why would I need to when I have a laptop?

I often wondered why computer labs still exist. It looks like I'm going to find out.

After typing in a passcode to one of the doors, Logan leads us into a small suite.

There are five computer screens and what look to be large old-school hard drives. The kind I've only seen on TV and on YouTube.

"What's the plan?" I ask while they're booting up two computers.

Angling back on the chair, looking so at ease you'd think he was about to launch into playing a video game, Ty smirks. "Using some skills that are going to be all levels of handy for my future career."

That's what I kind of figured. "But that's not

going to get us arrested, right?" Saying that— "If we get caught doing whatever it is we're doing, I'll shoulder it."

Not sure how the FBI would react to Ty getting a record.

"Puh-lease…," He drags out the word. "If I was to get caught, I'd have no right joining the FBI. We're not doing anything 'bad' per se." He totally air quotes. "More like tracking down a few names and wiping what the tech guys should have already taken down. Fucking amateurs."

"I'd like to think this is ethical tracing."

"Hacking," Ty corrects Logan with a smirk.

I am so here for this. "Fucking A. So, what's my job?"

Logan casts a small smile my way. "Coffee?"

That figures. "Fine. What do you want?"

WHAT I DON'T DO IS GO TO BOOK GRIND. IT'S OH SO tempting, though.

Instead, I'm a chickenshit and head to the small coffee cart to grab the guys' order. It's not as good as Tiller's coffee, but it'll give us all the caffeine fix we need.

"Okay, the site's down to the public, but we have

access to the backend so we can still follow the trail."

Ty lives for this shit.

He's far from a computer whiz. Okay, that's not technically true since he's a whiz at everything. More that cyber stuff isn't his passion. That he's dedicating his time to this by helping Tiller is as unsurprising as it is incredible.

"Weren't they all just student usernames?" I shrug, not sure what they're exactly hoping to track down. My username is LBrad34563, so even I can use the power of deduction to figure out the people behind the IDs.

"Not on this forum," Logan answers. "It's one that keeps popping up, and tech keeps shutting down, only for it to reappear again."

"Jesus, that sounds like a lot of effort and bullshit. Who has the time for that between studying and training? Hell, throw in a boyfriend and friends... I'm feeling time happy if I manage to take a shit without being interrupted."

Logan's lips twitch while Ty's still typing away and staring at a screen that technically I know is coding but looks more like an alien language.

"I suppose it's people who only have classes and none of the other three commits."

"Huh." I bob my head. "It makes sense. It would be boring as shit, I imagine."

"Anyway, regardless of why they do it, the usernames are set up to look like student logins. I suppose to provide a red herring of sorts."

"You know, 'red herring' was first used back in the fifteenth century, describing the smoking and salting of herring. It turned the white fish red. But it wasn't until a couple of hundred years later that it was first used like you're using it now. It was derived from breaking a fox's scent when training hunting dogs."

Both Logan and I stare at Ty. I'm so used to these moments of fact-sharing, I simply nod in acknowledgment, but I'm curious about Logan's reaction.

And damn if that isn't one loved-up expression.

He must have it bad if he finds Ty's random nuggets of knowledge endearing.

"So, you were saying?"

My words snap Logan out of the love-heart stare he's shooting at Ty. "Right, yes, so anyway, they look like the standard student logins, but they're not. It provided anonymity, hence the reason for such awful shit being said on there."

He's not wrong about it being awful. That's a pretty mild description, but still... it's fucking cowardly.

"Anonymity is an illusion." Ty doesn't stop what

he's doing, his fingers still flying over the keyboard. "You still need an email. There's still IP addresses."

"What about a free email provider, though? You don't need real details for those. Plus there's VPNs, right?"

"There's plenty of tech around to bypass the basic VPN bullshit. Plus, they'd need a super secure network. Most of the students in this place share data and rely on the school's shared Wi-Fi. So I'm banking on these guys not being smart enough to consider all those options. And certainly not flush with cash." He peers over at me and arches an eyebrow. "Arrogance breeds mistakes. They think they're untouchable. Invisible."

Damn... it's a hell of a thing being friends with Ty.

"But they're not," I answer.

"Damn straight they aren't."

A slow smile forms on my lips. Tiller is undoubtedly going to be hurt by this. I hate that. But at least we've taken it down and will have answers.

And I hope to god that Ty finds the evidence he needs to get Jones's ass off the team. And if the basketball gods are looking down on us, maybe out of school as well.

# CHAPTER 22
## TILLER

Confusion freezes my feet.

Dad's in the sitting room, Mom beside him on the couch, but it's Leon being here that's made me immobile.

"Hey," I manage. While it's good to see him, the expression on his face tells me this isn't a happy visit. I step fully into the room. "What's going on? Something's wrong." The statement is clear, as is my growing worry.

When Leon stands, a tentative smile on his face, my concern grows, lungs seizing. It's only him leaning into my space and pressing a tender, barely there kiss on my lips that has me breathing again.

Okay, so not here to break things off with me. Which would have been an odd thing to do with my parents being here, but rational thought when I'm on the cusp of a freak-out is never going to happen.

"Hey, your shift okay?" He worries his lip, his expression serious. There's a hesitant eagerness as he waits for me to answer.

"Yeah. Same old." It was a little quieter than usual, but that's not surprising since it's the time of year when students are slammed with assignments, so most aren't venturing out, even for a caffeine fix to keep them going.

I flick my gaze at my parents. Mom, well, she's trying to appear relaxed, but her ramrod-straight back shows she's anything but. Then there's Dad. He looks absolutely pissed off, but not with me, or even Leon.

If he was, I can't imagine Leon kissing me—however innocently—in front of my parents. It's something we've never done before, mainly because we're usually tucked away in his bedroom, but still.

"Someone want to tell me what's going on?"

Leon holds my hand and tugs me toward the second couch. It doesn't make me feel any less anxious.

"Seriously, you guys are beginning to freak me out."

Dad clearing his throat draws my attention. "Let's

preface this by saying it's been dealt with. The message board and the people responsible."

That doesn't sound good. There's an uptick in my pulse. It speeds through me like a freight train, tunneling through me so fast that, if I don't find out what the hell is going on, I'm either going to pass out or explode.

Maybe both.

"Dad, just tell me."

He bobs his head once. "There's been a forum feed, with you as the topic…"

And he goes on. Telling me everything that's been happening while I went about my shift making coffees, clearing up people's mess, and exchanging pleasantries.

The whole time Leon's gripping my hand. Mom is a silent force beside my dad.

No one interrupts. Not even me.

When he asks if I want to read the feed, look at it myself, I can't find the words. Instead, I shake my head. The thought of seeing them with my own eyes twists my gut too much, making all of this too real.

Then there's Davey's involvement. A cousin who I have little doubt I don't know. But that means nothing since Curtis still had a year left at college after I graduated, and apparently spilled his bullshit version of what went down.

The lies he will have told... the tales he likely spun.... Just the thought flips my nausea on its head and sears it with a fierce bolt of anger.

The motherfucker.

I'm starting to regret Dad not cutting off his dick right now.

And then there's Gavin Jones.

It's on the tip of my tongue to shout my incredulity. I've been helping the bastard on the court. Dedicating my time to him.

What an absolute piece-of-shit prick.

"Tyron gathered all the information. I've spoken to the dean."

I wince when I realize the scale of this.

"So everyone knows?" My voice feels scratchy. It's not been that long since I last spoke, but with emotion clogging my throat, it's amazing I can speak at all.

"Not everyone, no. It was only up for a couple of hours."

"Less than that," Leon says, squeezing my hand.

"And you have *nothing* to be ashamed of." The venom—all protective mama bear—in Mom's tone is enough to have my throat closing and tears welling. "You have done nothing wrong. You hear me? If anyone says anything to you or about you, they need a swift punch in the junk."

"*Mom.*" The word escapes on a laugh, momentarily shoving away my need to curl up into a ball and hide. Leon's snort closely follows.

"What? I'm deadly serious."

She is. Of that I have no doubt. Damn, I'm lucky to have her in my corner.

But fuck. This is all too much. A lead weight of dread clings to my mortification.

"Davey and Jones"—my voice remains scratchy, tired—"they're still on the team?"

It's been a long time since I've wanted to hide away. Three long years of finding myself, putting myself back together.

Logically, I know the only way to handle this is head-on. Just as I know adulting fucking sucks.

Logic doesn't stop my stomach from hurting, however.

Dad clenching his jaw gives me a bit of a warning.

"Davey still is, for now." His sigh is heavy. "While he brought the bullshit here, beyond gossiping, he's not broken any of Brixham's rules."

"But he hasn't exactly got the team's back either." Bitterness chases Leon's words.

While Dad doesn't answer with words, he dips his head in acknowledgment. He has to step carefully through this shitfest, I'm sure.

As my dad, he's outraged. As the head coach, he

needs to make sure he's following protocol and not accused of nepotism.

The reality is once again another hard slap in the face. How I got this job in the first place. How that could be perceived and misconstrued.

"I'll hand in my notice."

"No you damn well won't," Dad fires back. "You're doing great in the role."

"But all this is going to do is make things difficult for you, for Leon."

"Don't you even think about adding me to that list. I've held back from laying into Jones on more than one occasion for his shit talk about you." Surprise has my eyes widening. He has? But he doesn't stop. "You being an assistant coach doesn't make things harder for me. And your dad is right. You're fucking incredible."

The light chuckle from Dad cuts through the tension.

Leon's eyes widen, and he looks a bit panicked, red heating his cheeks. "Uhm, sorry, Coach, Mrs. Maple."

Since Dad looks proud and a soft smile plays on Mom's lips, I think he's got a pass for his cussing.

"Jones is off the team."

With a rush of relief, my breath whooshes out of me.

"I was able to argue the case for his removal based on the illegal forum he was involved in and on the grounds of his failure to meet our program's expectations. A direct attack on an assistant coach, in writing, plus a handful of additional concerns from the coaching staff were more than enough to make it happen."

"And he won't contest it?"

Dad shakes his head. "The dean's word is final. He supported me with this 100 percent. It helped that because his recent request for additional time with you was granted, something I didn't even need to agree to but did so anyway, his actions were even more of a concern. We hold high standards for all our players. What he did is a direct violation of those standards."

I bob my head.

"Jones has already been told. Davey's been told in no uncertain terms that if he doesn't get his shit together and work for the good of the team, he's out."

Jesus.

Sure, I'm relieved, but I hate that any of this has happened. I'm livid, too, but more than that, I'm dog-tired.

"Honey, why don't we talk more about this in the morning, okay? You don't have to be at practice again until tomorrow night, so you have some time to rest. We're here tomorrow morning for you if you want to talk this out." Mom flicks her gaze to Leon. "You're more than welcome to stay the night."

I angle toward Leon, my heart warming at the light pink crawling up his neck. He turns to me, a silent question in his gaze.

"Yeah. Stay?"

"Of course. Whatever you need."

I stand, needing to escape into my room just as much as I want to hide away in the comfort of Leon's arms.

Not releasing my hand, Leon follows suit. We say goodnight to my folks, me giving them each a one-armed hug, accepting their love as I tell them thanks.

Once we're in my room, I fall back on my bed, tugging Leon with me. He shuffles around so my head's on his chest and I'm wrapped up in his strong arms.

"You know this is going to be okay, right? I'm not saying it's not shit, but I've got your back. So does the team."

I sigh into his hold. "Tyron and Logan really got all that information on Jones?"

A quiet chuckle flows out of Leon. "They sure did. Ty lives for this shit. Plus, he's protective of you."

That should sound ridiculous. I'm older and have a position of responsibility, but over the past few months I've gotten to know Tyron well. I don't need clarity about why I'm included in the fierce protective streak he has.

I nod, a deep yawn wrenching from me. Exhaustion beats at my heels, making my eyelids droop.

"Let's get undressed and into bed." Leon's already moving, helping me strip. He's gentle in his actions. We've torn each other's clothes off several times over the past few months, but this is so different.

Tender fingers help me. Care is in each touch, and when he covers us up with my blankets that smell of home and comfort, a content sigh passes my lips. By the morning, they'll smell of Leon too.

"Thank you for staying."

A soft kiss is pressed against my head.

"You don't need to thank me. You hurting is not okay."

My heart flips. "You said earlier, you've had to hold back a few times with Jones?" There's clear question in my tone. He's never mentioned anything before.

Arms squeezing me tighter, he presses another kiss to the top of my head. "He's been pushing my buttons for a while. Talking shit. It's been difficult, but I handled my reaction. Just."

I tilt my head, my cheek still on his shoulder, but enough that I can meet his eyes. "You didn't tell me."

He shakes his head. "It's not been easy separating my feelings for my boyfriend from one of my assistant coaches. Making sure I try to behave the same way to you as anyone else."

For me either. It's partly why I didn't complain to Dad about spending more time with Jones when Leon was the person to really benefit from the specialized shooter coaching.

"Is it too hard?"

At his quirked brow, I huff out a laugh and roll my eyes. That he's made me laugh when I'm so drained is a hell of a thing.

"Not your dick." My lips twitch. "Me being on the coaching team? Has it made life difficult for you?"

"Fuck no. Come here."

I scoot up so my head's on the pillow and we're facing each other.

"My training is more rigorous than ever before. You being there motivates me. Is making me a better player. We are going to dominate next month when games finally start."

It's a relief to have that confirmed. Heat also warms my neck from his praise.

The click of his swallow jerks my attention to his throat before we make eye contact.

"I love you. Having your support this season means everything. I just hope I can give just as much support as you give me."

My breath catches as my pulse shoots off into the stratosphere.

And I'm moving.

I capture his lips, pouring everything I feel for this man into the kiss. We kiss until I'm dizzy. We kiss until we're both panting. We kiss until I'm so fucking hard that my dick might explode.

But first….

I pull away gasping, my breaths choppy. "I love you. So fucking much."

The biggest of smiles transforms his lust-addled face. The pink dots on his cheeks bloom, and still he's grinning.

"How about I give you an I-love-you bj, but only if you can keep quiet?"

At his dancing eyebrows, I snicker, my dick throbbing in expectation.

"How about we take this to the shower so I can hear your moans when you come down my throat after?" I counter.

Wide-eyed, Leon almost knees me in the groin with the haste of clambering out of bed.

A laugh loud spills out of me, happiness expanding my chest and love settling in so deeply I know whatever happens tomorrow is going to be okay.

It's impossible for it not to be. Not when Leon loves me and has my back, no matter what happens.

# CHAPTER 23
## LEON

Having asked Tyron to fill our housemates in on all that had happened, I step into the locker room with a smile and only a bit of tension.

I haven't seen anyone all day, beyond Sammy in one of our lectures.

I set my alarm early this morning to work on the joint project I'd missed out on yesterday. Somehow amid the drama, I remembered to send off an apology, a request to add everything to a shared document, and a promise to catch up and not let anyone down.

Thank fuck the group members are understanding.

It does mean any spare time I had today was spent either checking in on Tiller or scrambling to work on the project.

Fatigue is not my friend. Between lack of sleep and my worry, my whole focus now is getting through practice, ideally without incident.

What I haven't heard, though, is any gossip.

Maybe that's because more and more people are discovering who my boyfriend is, so I'm not in the loop. What I hope, though, is that the few members involved—all who Ty tracked—were pulled in to see the dean this morning.

As far as I'm aware, only Davey and Jones were called in last night.

I've not seen or heard a peep out of either.

"Yo, Leon," Kieran calls as soon as my feet touch tile, "tell Banks here about the no-look behind-the-back pass you did in that game against Bryant."

I smirk as I step farther into the room. Shoving my bag in my cubby, I look Banks's way. He's midway through tying his sneakers, but his attention is on me, clearly waiting for me to follow through.

I roll my eyes good-naturedly, silently thanking Kieran for handling my entrance this way. "The one where I was making a fast break?" A glance at Kieran, who nods and follows up with a wink, and I chuckle. "Yeah." I carve my fingers through my mess of hair. "Not sure I'll be able to get away with that move again."

I proceed to tell Banks, and anyone who's bothering to listen, about when I drove toward the basket, the whole defense on my ass. It was then I faked a pass to Ty with a behind-the-back move. It was pretty damn audacious, but fuck if we weren't all surprised that it worked.

The ball, rather than going to Ty, flew to Kieran instead. He hadn't been expecting it at all. I can still remember the surprise on his face, right along with him hauling ass on the fly and scoring an easy layup.

By the time I'm finished, Jacobs, the sophomore who joined us this year, is chuckling and looking for the footage on YouTube. We're all snickering about the ploy, Sammy getting overzealous by thinking of other moves we could fake to get the opposition spiraling, when Coach enters the locker room.

The room quiets immediately.

During training, Coach rarely ventures in the locker room, no doubt enjoying the freedom of talking to us on the court, well away from the stench in here.

At his tail are the four assistant coaches on staff. Tiller included.

For the first time, I glance fully around the locker room, seeking Davey out.

Sitting on the bench, his face pointed at the floor, he clasps his hands together. They're so tight, his dark skin pales.

I can't help the clenching of my jaw or the rush of anger that he brought the gossip to our locker room.

A nudge at my side from Kieran has me pulling my attention away. It settles on Tiller. Our gazes connect, and while he doesn't smile, his eyes tell me enough.

He loves me and wants to know if I'm okay.

It's almost comical, his concern for me, when he's the one dealing with the fallout.

I offer a slight up-nod, pouring my emotions for him into my gaze, hoping he can feel just how incredible I think he is. The barely there uplift of his lips is just for me, then gone in the next second before his attention drifts away.

Loosening my shoulders, I fold my arms, stance wide, perhaps just a little defensive as I focus on Coach.

"Listen up." His tone's hard but not angry. It's one that tells us what he has to say is serious and needs to be listened to carefully, if we know what's good for us.

There's no shuffling of feet, no soft murmurs. Beyond the sound of breathing, it would still be possible to hear a pin drop.

"Today we're one Bears member short."

From the lack of gasping or even reaction, it's clear everyone at least noticed Jones's absence.

"This is the one and only time I expect to have to say this. It's certainly the only time I want to hear this mentioned again," he starts, his gaze flinty as he takes us all in. "We play as a team, on and off the court. That means you meet my expectations every practice and game. Every time you're in this locker room, you're representing the team. Every time you're on campus or knocking back tequila shots, *you* are representing the team. That means you defend one another, have one another's backs. That means you shut down any gossip, any misinformation someone is foolish enough to be spreading. Failure to do that is a direct reflection of your character. Failure to do that is a direct violation of your agreement to be a team player. It's disrespectful to your team-mates, to me, to your coaches, to your fans. Understood?"

A chorus of "Yes, Coach" rings out.

Coach's gaze narrows as he takes us in. After a few more painfully intense seconds, he bobs his head. "Two minutes to get your asses on the court." He turns and leaves. The assistant coaches follow, gazes fixed with similar expressions to Coach's.

There's a moment of stillness. An uncertainty in the air.

Sammy's deep "I don't have friends. I've got

family" echoes around the locker room. A grin splits his mouth as he shoots me a wink and claps Banks on the back.

Multiple snorts and chuckles follow.

"Okay, *Dom*." Kieran rolls his eyes at Sammy, but like me, I know he's grateful for Sammy cutting through the tension. "You heard the coach." Kieran moves toward the exit and stops before leaving, turning to face us. "Get your asses moving. Show him we're the team to be proud of. The team who won the championship last year and can do so again."

"Yeehaw, motherfuckers!" Sammy hollers as he jogs past Kieran. The team follows suit—with the jogging rather than the yelling.

I hold back, as does Davey.

Kieran arches his brow at me, and I indicate for him to leave us. He does so without a backward glance.

Finally, Davey looks at me. I have no compassion for the worry in his gaze or the nerves keeping his body locked up. He's lucky he's here.

"Let me get something straight," I start. I don't get into his face, not sure I'll trust myself if there's even the slightest hint of defiance or a sneer. "At the moment, no one wants you here." Fuck if I care that

I'm being cruel. I'm saying it as it is. He blanches. "That doesn't mean you can't make amends and prove you deserve a place on the team."

Surprise registers, and he stutters out a heavy breath.

I know. I didn't realize how magnanimous I could be either.

"If you want to be here, don't fuck with us."

"I won't. I'm sorry. I didn't even think—"

I shake my head, not wanting to hear it.

"Sure, the coaches can piss us off sometimes. Hell, so can some of the guys, but we still keep our shit together and have each other's backs. You stabbed us in ours when you decided to talk shit about not only one of the coaches but my boyfriend."

From the widening of his eyes, it's new information to him. Huh, perhaps we've been doing a better job at being subtle than I thought.

"I didn't k—"

I shake my head, cutting him off again. "That he is hit a little deeper, but we all would have reacted the same even if it was Coach Norris or anyone else."

"Yeah." He nods. "I hear you."

I study him a beat. He seriously has been a wallflower so far this training season, but there has to be something about him that's brought him here. No way Coach would have given him a chance otherwise.

"Good. Now, get your ass on the court and train till you feel like you're going to die, then push some more. It's the only way your feet will ever find court time."

With another nod, he races on past, leaving me alone and breathing heavily.

Jesus, that was hard, giving the fucker a chance like that.

"Hey."

Tiller's voice has me spinning in his direction.

"I didn't see any bloody noses or swollen eyes." His lips twitch. "It's also hella sweet what you said to him. How you defended me."

I step into his space. At the moment I don't care about our rules and maintaining professionalism. "You heard that?"

His nod is slow, sultry as he latches on to my waist and hauls me toward him. I go willingly. I always will.

"You doing okay? Anything happen today?"

"You mean since the last time you checked in on me?" he teases.

I shrug, not at all ashamed that I've been annoying him with my calls. Worry makes me extra needy apparently.

"And no. Not really. A couple of second looks. Nothing I can't handle. Heard Jones has left, though."

"No shit!" Glee has me smiling. "That was fast."

"I imagine he's organized a transfer, probably a school in desperate need of quality players."

I scrunch my nose, hating the fact that Jones actually is a skilled player. My brows lift in realization.

"What?"

"Let's just hope he transfers to a West Coast team, and we can kick his ass in a game."

Tiller snorts. "You're incorrigible."

"Only when it matters."

His gaze is soft, full of what I now know is love.

"We best get going."

I nod, reluctantly agreeing. "Not sure I have the energy for Coach to be pissed at my tardiness."

"True that." He punctuates his words with a gentle kiss. It's enough to send a buzz of energy zipping through my veins.

I smile as I pull back and turn to jog away, not lying about the real concern of Coach adding time to drills. There's a smack on my ass and I snort out a laugh, then peer over my shoulder for one last look.

Tiller's heated eyes are on me. Full of promise and emotion for everything I know he'll whisper sweetly in my ear when we're wrapped around each other in my bed.

I turn back, a giant grin stretching my lips and my heart so full I know the rest of the year is going to be pretty damn spectacular. That, and if I have my way, so will the rest of our lives together.

# EPILOGUE
## TILLER

"Go ask Meemaw Julie."

Leon's mom is knee-deep in making cookies. Henry's already helping her, but little Ethan got distracted a while ago. Since he's now bored again and I'm tired of pulling rocks from his chubby hands that he keeps on licking, I have no guilt in passing him off to his meemaw.

At my side, my husband snorts, but I don't look his way just yet, my gaze trailing after Ethan as he totters his two-year-old feet along the short path and through the open patio door into the kitchen.

"Subtle."

I arch an eyebrow at Leon. He's all smirk and a little glassy eyed from his third beer. Yeah, we've turned into total lightweights since becoming dads of two energetic boys. Henry, at four, is a little easier to handle, while Ethan keeps us constantly on our toes.

"What, I didn't see you battling our two-year-old for dominion over the rocks. I can get him back if you want."

Still smirking, he stretches out on the wicker chair. The movement tugs up his shirt, revealing a delicious sliver of skin. His chuckle pulls my attention to his face.

"You know, with the kids distracted and my parents taking care of them, you can suck my dick if you want."

Entertained by his lack of filter—I always am when he's horny drunk—I snort. "That's a super tempting offer, baby."

"But perhaps not something you should be offering in front of your father-in-law."

"Oh fuck." Leon jerks so fast, wide-eyed and horror-stricken, he topples the chair, falling backward into the flower bed with an *"Oomph."*

I jump up, laughing while making sure he hasn't done any damage to himself. Peering down at him sprawled in the flower bed, crushing his mom's asters squashed under his ass, I grin. "You okay down there?"

At my words, he arches his brow, a tease on his

lips. Since his mind's totally gone in a hot and dirty direction, I figure he'll live.

"Let's get you up before your mom comes out and threatens you with a spatula." Grasping his hand, I tug him to standing. When he's in my arms, I dot my lips to his and pull a purple flower from his hair.

"Looks like you've been starting the party without me."

We shift our attention to Dad. He's wearing a Lions jersey, identical to mine and Leon's, total courtesy of Kieran.

"Hey, Coach."

My lips twitch. Leon has never broken the habit of calling Dad anything but his moniker.

"Bradford," Dad greets.

I step away from Leon so I can greet Dad properly with a hug. Leon follows suit before we head inside, searching for Mom. That my folks are here means the game's about to start.

I check on the boys, scooping Ethan up and blowing a raspberry on his stomach. The squeal close to my ear is totally worth it. Our boys' laughter is the best sound ever.

"You ready to watch the game? See Uncle Kieran win the playoffs?"

Ethan bobs his head, and he snuggles onto my lap

as I sit down next to Leon. Henry's on his lap, also wearing Kieran's jersey. He also has what I think is meant to be a lion painted on his face.

"Nice artwork."

Henry peers up at me wearing a wide grin so similar to his dad's that it makes my heart pulse with love. "Meemaw did it. It the same as Unca Key's lion."

"It looks awesome. Let me take a picture to send to Uncle Dean."

Henry poses for a photograph, which I shoot off to Dean. I know he'll get a kick out of Henry's excitement.

While we don't get that much chance to catch up with any of the guys in person, we're still tight. Plus, it's the offseason soon—well, technically as soon as this game is over. It means life's easier for Keiran and Dean, and for me.

The summer break is almost over, and I'll be heading back to work at Barth's College as head coach in a few weeks, but that gives us enough time to catch up with the guys. A yearly tradition no one's bailed on yet.

"Daddy, youse gots purple flowers in your hair."

Leon chuckles as Henry eyes the squashed flowers.

"Are those my asters?" His mom's eyeing him,

and I tug my lips between my teeth to stop myself from laughing.

"Hmm… what?"

Leon sucks at acting casual.

"If that bed's not immaculate, you're going to find yourself here next week replanting."

Leon sighs, turning into the younger version of himself—the one I first met and fell in love with seven years ago. "Yes, Mom."

"Ooh, if you're doing Julie's, maybe next time you visit, you can build me a new flower bed under the kitchen window." Mom, as swift as ever, ends with a sly grin.

Dad chuckles as he steps into the room, sweeping Ethan out of my arms. "I'll make sure I've organized the timber and the compost for your visit."

Leon narrows his gaze at our parents. There's no disguising his amusement, though, nor his absolute love for everyone in the room. "I suppose you want me to open up my calendar to you all so you can organize future projects and bookings."

"That's a great idea." His mom winks at me as she accepts a glass of wine from George, Leon's dad.

Leon tuts, offering me a sweet smile. "I'm just thinking all these jobs provide ample babysitting opportunities." His voice is low. His words are also bullshit.

We've had a total of two nights at home kid free so far. Leon is even more reluctant to have time out than I am, and that's saying something. Though, to be fair, my time away during the season makes me frustratingly used to not being with my boys.

Leon, though, took time off when both boys were born. He's been working part-time from home ever since. He may consider taking on more as the boys get older, but at the moment, it works for us.

It's even more helpful that his parents sold up and moved closer to us. One of his sisters too.

"Whatever you say, baby," I agree. Maybe we should make that happen soon. Just the thought of his earlier offer of a bj is enough to make me think about the luxury of an uninterrupted night together.

Though, knowing us, we'll probably crash early and sleep through till noon. As long as Leon's in my arms the whole night, it definitely sounds like a win.

George turns up the volume on the flatscreen as the players start to warm up.

I grin, sinking into the couch as Leon wraps an arm around my shoulders, Henry still on his lap. I sneak a sly look in Leon's direction, taking in his profile.

He's still as kissable as ever.

That was as clear to me from the moment my eyes landed on his as it is right now.

His gaze meets mine, and he tilts his head, question in his eyes. Whatever he sees in mine, he responds to, his attention briefly dipping to my mouth.

"I'll always only want your kisses." His soft tone wraps around the words.

I don't say a thing. I don't need to.

Instead, I brush my lips lightly across his before scooting even closer.

This right here is more than I ever hoped for in life.

I just know each day is going to keep getting better and better.

***

WANT TO GET UP CLOSE AND PERSONAL WITH OTHER Bears players? Check out more books in the Fast Break series with Kieran's story in RULES, SCHMULES! and Tyron's story in FACTS, SMACTS!

Don't worry, Sammy will be getting his story too. You can preorder EASY, SCHMEASY HERE!

If you're looking for the "sort of" grown-up basketball players, then check out my Zone Defense series, starting with the bestseller NO TAKE BACKS.

# ACKNOWLEDGMENTS

As always, my team of editors, Kristin, Liv, Donna, and Jamee, deserve so much thanks and credit. You really are incredible.

Claire from BookSmith Designs reads my mind every single time. I'm so blessed to have your support.

A special thanks to Barb and CC, who work tirelessly behind the scenes supporting me.

A HUGE thanks to my group, RoMMance with Becca and Louisa, for your fun interactions and daily support, and obviously my bestie Louisa for keeping me entertained.

# ABOUT THE AUTHOR

I live and breathe all things book related. Usually with at least three books being read and two WiPs being written at the same time, life is merrily hectic. I tend to do nothing by halves, so I happily seek the craziness and busyness life offers.

Living on my small property in Queensland with my human family as well as my animal family of cows, sheep, chooks, and dogs, I really do appreciate the beauty of the world around me and am a believer that love truly is love.

To check for updates head to my website:
https://beccaseymour.com
https://landing.mailerlite.com/webforms/
landing/r9f0i4
Plus, join my Facebook group, which I share with the awesome Louisa Masters here:
https://www.facebook.com/groups/
rommancewithbeccalouisa/

facebook.com/beccaseymourauthor

twitter.com/beccaseymour_

instagram.com/authorbeccaseymour

bookbub.com/authors/becca-seymour

tiktok.com/@beccaseymourwrites